Kiss The Flame

Also from Christopher Rice

Thrillers
A DENSITY OF SOULS
THE SNOW GARDEN
LIGHT BEFORE DAY
BLIND FALL
THE MOONLIT EARTH

Supernatural Thrillers
THE HEAVENS RISE
THE VINES

Paranormal Romance
THE FLAME: A Desire Exchange Novella
THE SURRENDER GATE: A Desire Exchange Novel

Kiss The Flame

A Desire Exchange Novella

By Christopher Rice

1001 Dark Nights

Kiss The Flame
A Desire Exchange Novella
By Christopher Rice

1001 Dark Nights

Print ISBN: 978-1-940887-75-3

Published by Evil Eye Concepts, Incorporated

Acknowledgments

I feel like I've found a new family at 1,001 Dark Nights. I can't thank my fellow series authors enough for all they've done to welcome me into the world of romance. After years of publishing dark thrillers, it was time to try something different, something new. Something with a happier ending, and Liz Berry, M.J. Rose, and Jillian Stein not only made that possible, but rewarding.

Kimberly and "Shy Pam", you ladies are the best. Kasi, you're a great copyeditor and Asha, you're one of the best cover designers at work today. Period.

A big thank you to K.P. Simmons and Inkslinger P.R. as well.

Thanks also to my crew at The Dinner Party Show, in particular my best friend and co-host Eric Shaw Quinn, for making it possible to meet my writing deadlines while also producing a weekly live Internet radio broadcast. Ben Scuglia provided additional copyediting for which I'm very grateful.

A big thank you to everyone at The Montelone Hotel in New Orleans for making it such a special place to stay every time I visit. I hope you're happy with how you're portrayed in these pages. And I hope Lilliane figures out a way to conceal her identity so she can keep reserving a room there for many books to come. In fact, let me get to work on that one right now.

Sign up for the 1001 Dark Nights Newsletter
and be entered to win a Tiffany Key necklace.

There's a contest every month!

Go to www.1001DarkNights.com to subscribe.

As a bonus, all subscribers will receive a free
1001 Dark Nights story
The First Night
by Lexi Blake & M.J. Rose

One Thousand and One Dark Nights

Once upon a time, in the future…

I was a student fascinated with stories and learning. I studied philosophy, poetry, history, the occult, and the art and science of love and magic. I had a vast library at my father's home and collected thousands of volumes of fantastic tales.

I learned all about ancient races and bygone times. About myths and legends and dreams of all people through the millennium. And the more I read the stronger my imagination grew until I discovered that I was able to travel into the stories... to actually become part of them.

I wish I could say that I listened to my teacher and respected my gift, as I ought to have. If I had, I would not be telling you this tale now.
But I was foolhardy and confused, showing off with bravery.

One afternoon, curious about the myth of the Arabian Nights, I traveled back to ancient Persia to see for myself if it was true that every day Shahryar (Persian: شهریار, "king") married a new virgin, and then sent yesterday's wife to be beheaded. It was written and I had read, that by the time he met Scheherazade, the vizier's daughter, he'd killed one thousand women.

Something went wrong with my efforts. I arrived in the midst of the story and somehow exchanged places with Scheherazade – a phenomena that had never occurred before and that still to this day, I cannot explain.

Now I am trapped in that ancient past. I have taken on Scheherazade's life and the only way I can protect myself and stay alive is to do what she did to protect herself and stay alive.

Every night the King calls for me and listens as I spin tales. And when the evening ends and dawn breaks, I stop at a point that leaves him breathless and yearning for more. And so the King spares my life for one more day, so that he might hear the rest of my dark tale.

As soon as I finish a story... I begin a new one... like the one that you, dear reader, have before you now.

THE CANDLEMAKER

We see ghosts every day; we just don't realize it.

The woman a few feet behind you on the street corner, for instance, the one who doesn't quite belong. Maybe she gazes at you with too much interest and seems unaffected by the commotion surrounding you both. When you turn to look at her a second time, she vanishes, leaving you to wonder if she was a trick of your imagination or if she merged so quickly with the crowd of pedestrians surging through the intersection you just lost track of her.

This is how we see ghosts—often and without our knowledge.

They don't appear to us in states of dismemberment or disarray, leering at us like horror movie ghouls. They are not tricksters, not demons. Rather, they have been chosen by forces beyond our comprehension to remain among the living. But to qualify for this privilege, they must possess an undeniable respect, an undeniable *love,* for human beings. Only then will the spirit world see fit to grant them a particular purpose that justifies their continued visits to our mortal plane.

For years now people in the French Quarter have caught glimpses of a handsome, elegantly dressed man who takes long walks in the rain, his silk vests and perfectly pressed slacks bone-dry underneath the purple bloom of his umbrella. But glimpses are all they get. If someone's curious look turns into a lingering stare, if their expression becomes suspicious, this man employs the favored trick of all ghosts; he halts the clock of human experience and quickens his steps until he's found a comfortable distance between himself and his suspicious observer. Then he releases his grip on what we ordinary mortals call seconds and minutes.

The same can be said for those who walk past his tiny shop in the middle of the day, its plate glass windows filled with shelves holding rows of fat candles in burnt umber glass containers. At first glance, they assume the place is closed because the items inside are so expensive, potential customers must make an appointment to gain admittance. But this ludicrous proposition— how expensive can a candle be, really?—doesn't hold them for more than a few steps. When they turn to get a second look, the store and its contents have vanished without a trace, leaving them convinced their passing glimpse of purple wax was just a trick of the mind.

But the shop's tiny front door does open for a select few. To these people, a wood plank, hand-painted sign appears over the entrance, bearing the outline of a small gold flame, and the shop's name, *Feu du Coeur*. They are drawn through the shop's entrance by a smell so overpowering it brings tears of gratitude to their eyes or a lustful quickening to their pulse. For them, the light within looks inviting and warm, and the man waiting for them inside, the same man who takes long walks in the rain under his purple umbrella, offers them not only his name, Bastian Drake, but a chance to change their lives forever.

1

LANEY

Before college, Laney didn't believe men like Michael Brouchard existed, men who look brawny enough to play for the NFL but spend their days leading passionate discussions of paintings like *The Kiss* by Gustav Klimt. Men who don't trip over the pronunciation of words like *mélange* and *rococo*, who combine their fierce intelligence with artfully tousled dark hair and thick-framed glasses that make them look like Clark Kent. Men with strong, veiny, muscular forearms dusted with light tufts of hair. Forearms they keep exposed by rolling the sleeves of their plaid shirts up just far enough to offer teasing glimpses to their admiring students, glimpses that leave those students, students like Laney Foley, wondering what it would feel like to have those powerful hands slide up their thighs, grasping, kneading, before their owner leans in all professor-like and asks if he can—

"Miss Foley?"

"Sure," Laney grunts.

"*Sure*?"

"I mean…yes…"

A ripple of laughter spreads through the tiny classroom. Laney's cheeks flame. There are only ten other students in her discussion section for Foundations of Western Art II, but she's convinced they're all peering into her mind and tittering over the dirty thoughts she's been having about their TA.

The Kiss fills the pull-screen across the room, a patchwork of gold and other bright colors framing the placid facial expression of a beautiful young woman held in her lover's firm, upright embrace. Its image is cast by the digital projector sitting a few feet from where Michael has been pacing for most of class. Something about all that glittering eroticism in the same small classroom as her handsome young professor has sent her on a fantasy spiral and now she can barely recover.

He's not a professor, she reminds herself. *Not technically. He's a grad student. A teaching assistant. Just a few years older than me.* The real reason for the slight age difference between them is not something Laney wants to share with her classmates. Most of them drive cars with monthly notes three times her parent's mortgage. God forbid she get branded the girl from Lafourche Parish who had to bust her hump in community college for two years before she could land a scholarship good enough to cover the cost of tuition here.

"In 1894, Gustav Klimt was commissioned to create three paintings to decorate the ceiling of the Great Hall at the University of Vienna," her teacher says. "I asked you what year those paintings were destroyed."

"1945," Laney says.

"*Meeeaaaaaah,*" erupts the Hollister-clad frat boy a few desks away. It's the guy's best vocal impersonation of a wrong answer buzzer from a game show, and he inflicts it on them all at least twice a class. In high school, Jake Briffel was probably the kid who spent most of his time shoving smaller kids into lockers. Now he brandishes the one weapon a bully can still get away with using once they reach college—his mouth. So far, all of Laney's discussion sections have offered up some version of a Jake Briffel, and she's been pretty good at ignoring most of them.

"Listen to the question, genius," Jake says. "Klimt got the commission in eighteen ninety-four. You really think they would have waited a whole decade to deploy his art?"

Ugh, Laney thinks. *Why'd he have to make it so easy? I totally could have ignored him if he hadn't made it so—*

"Actually," Laney says. "His question was when were the paintings *destroyed*, not *deployed*. Because we're talking about art. Not soldiers. You probably got confused because the paintings were destroyed by the Nazis when they retreated from Vienna. Which happened in 1945. As I just said."

Jake's anger radiates like the heat of a small fire. She could care less. She's too stricken by the expression on her teacher's face.

Maybe Michael Brouchard is proud of her. It's probably the most she's said in class this whole year. But do you moisten your bottom lip with the tip of your tongue and then bite it gently and pretty much look like you're about to spread someone across your desk just 'cause you're feeling proud of them?

"Thanks, scholarship," Jake snarls. "I'm sure your Nazi history will go over big with the other lunch ladies at the caff." He caps off this insult with a contorted facial expression meant to imply that *lunch ladies* are by their very nature mentally challenged.

She should laugh it off. But the twofold insult—the reference to both her scholarship and her work study hours—catches her so off guard she finds herself blinking madly, suddenly terrified that she might be on the verge of stunned tears, as if Jake's words had the force of a literal slap.

How did he find out about her scholarship? Silly of her to think somebody wouldn't eventually. Most colleges are like small towns, she figures, just another place where a secret can only be kept for a day. Why should Chamberland University be any different? And it hasn't been the easiest—slinging meatloaf and spoonfuls of brown rice for the few freshman stuck on meal plan. But it's a job like any other, and God knows, she's had worse jobs. Graveyard shift at a gas station on the West Bank; busser at a French Quarter nightclub where she was too young to serve drinks but old enough to have her ass grabbed by an endless stream of conventioneers. But Briffel's cruel joke has her suddenly convinced everyone in school's been laughing at her under their breath as they carry their trays to their tables. *Look at the sophomore who's three years older than the other sophomores. The one whose mother used to shuck oysters for a living before she keeled over dead at thirty-one. The one who stays up late mixing cheap drug store moisturizers together 'till she's got a recipe as potent as whatever top brand moisturizer the other girls here are using to look like runway models at eight in the frickin' morning.*

She stops blinking. Her vision clears, thank God, leaving her with strained breaths and a rushing sound in her ears.

When she looks up, she finds herself staring into her teacher's eyes. She's never found anger beautiful before, but that's the only word she can think of to describe the rage that's hardened Michael Brouchard's features into statuesque angles. He's been studying her, taking in the physical signs of how deeply Briffel's comment wounded her, and when he shifts his focus from her to Briffel, Laney hears the sound of a gun cocking somewhere in her mind.

"Mr. Briffel," Michael says. "Since we're all speaking so freely now apparently, allow me to take this moment to tell you how impressed I am with the speed at which you Google the answers to most of my questions on your phone underneath your desk. However, I'm a bit concerned that even those assignments for which you are given adequate time to prepare are also reading like you just Googled a bunch of crap on your phone under your desk. So with that in mind, I have the following suggestion. If you would like to place your focus on those classmates of yours who are working *a lot* harder than you are, perhaps you should take what you see there as motivation for something other than an inappropriate comment which could result in a reduction of your grade."

"You can't do that," Briffel whines. "You can't reduce my grade just 'cause I made a *joke*."

"Try me," Michael Brouchard says. It's not quite a growl, but it's close enough to one that Laney can almost smell fur.

Michael rests both fists on the front edge of Jake Briffel's desk. The frat boy stares up at him slack-jawed, too frightened to come up with his next move or even a passable response.

Laney wouldn't be surprised to see a wet spot in the dude's pants.

Lord knows, there's about to be one in hers, although of a different origin.

Briffel's been a jerk from day one, but he's never been quite this mean to anyone in class before now. Maybe that's the only reason their teacher went after him with such focused, passionate anger. But when Michael turns away from Briffel's desk, his eyes meet hers for a telling instant. Just long enough to tell her he's got her back. Just long enough to suggest his thoughts about her might be as full of passion and abandon as the thoughts she's been having about him.

Laney's no stranger to lust. She is, however, a stranger to gorgeous, intelligent men leaping to her defense. The combination of the two not only makes her head spin, it makes the memory of Briffel's cruel joke feel as distant as China.

"Laney?"

Michael's call halts her steps and sends gooseflesh racing up her back. It sounds like he's only a few feet away, which means he must have rushed out of class with most of the other students in order to catch up with her. Two urges battle for control of her legs—the urge to run like hell, and the urge to fall to her knees on the sidewalk in a gesture of total worship as he approaches.

"Too much?" Michael asks once he's a few feet away.

He's winded, she realizes. *He* did *run to catch up with me.* The thought of him giving the brush-off to other students as he slipped from the classroom in pursuit makes her feel both giddy and guilty.

It's a crisp fall day in New Orleans, just cool enough for a light, hooded sweater like the one he clearly slid on in a hurry given how unevenly it sits across his shoulders. Sunlight bounces off the tinted windows of The Jillian Stein Arts Center behind him, making the trees that surround the building look like they're on fire. It lances the oak branches overhead, a shaft of it falling across his right eye, causing the hazel iris to shimmer in a way that makes her gasp.

She'd never thought of a man as being *beautiful* before she met Michael. Plenty of guys she'd met were hot, handsome, or *ruggedly handsome*, that special third category she used to define edgy, unconventional sex appeal. But something about his combination of hard angles and lingering, thoughtful expressions, of determined masculinity matched with a gentle, careful demeanor—beautiful is the only word she can think of to describe those contradictions and the effect they have on her pulse. And it's the only word she can literally think as he stares into her eyes, waiting for a response to his cryptic question.

"I'm sorry," she finally says. "Too much? What do you mean?"

"Some students, they don't like it when…you know, a teacher kind of steps up to bat for them. It makes them feel—"

"Nice?" she says before she can stop herself.

At first, it looks like her answer has made him wince. But after another second or two, it's clear Michael is fighting a smile so strong it looks ready to conquer his face. But he's fighting it, that's for sure. Because the fact that he made her feel *nice* pleases him, and it pleases him a little more than a teacher should be pleased by his student.

"Or nice," he finally says.

"I appreciated it. Honestly."

"Well, you know, Jake is such a jerk and—wow. I shouldn't be saying that. Sorry. I shouldn't be talking about another student that way. I shouldn't…"

And suddenly he's lost his grip on his words and his eyes are roaming her body as if he's thinking all sorts of things about it he shouldn't. And she can feel Michael, the guy who's only three years older than she is, fighting with Mr. Brouchard, the guy who's supposed to be her teacher, the guy who's probably signed some sort of contract that says he won't do any of the things he's thinking about doing to her right now with any student ever.

"You make me say things I shouldn't, Laney Foley."

"Make you?"

"Sorry. That's not exactly fair, I guess."

"You apologize a lot when we're not in class, Mr. Brouchard."

"Yeah, well, whatever I did to make you call me Mr. Brouchard, I apologize."

"You're right. Jake is a jerk."

"Still, I shouldn't have said it..."

"The thing in class?"

"No. Just now. When I called him a jerk. The thing in class? If you're good with it, I'm good with it. Because to be honest, that was the only thing that mattered to me. That you were good with it."

"I'm very good with it," she says. It feels like she spoke in almost a whisper, but Michael nods like he's heard her clearly.

"A couple weeks into semester, you went quiet. I wasn't sure what happened. But I missed you. I missed your contributions, I mean, and today, when you spoke up again, I was so happy, I wasn't about to let Jake Briffel scare you into hiding again."

"Hiding?" She hates the defensive tone in her voice. "I've got perfect attendance. For the discussions and the lectures."

"There are lots of ways to hide."

"Still..."

"I didn't mean to offend you."

"No, it's just... I'm not like a lot of the students here, Michael."

"Yeah, I know. You're better than most of them."

"Well, no, I just meant that—thank you, by the way, for saying that—but what I meant was when I first got here I was kind of...Well, I was kind of a bitch."

"Not in class, you weren't," he says.

"Everywhere else I was. I guess because I'm one of the *lunch ladies*. I was expecting people to reject me right off so I thought I'd beat them to the punch by speaking my mind even when they didn't really ask me to."

"What's wrong with speaking your mind?"

"Well, for instance, if I gave you my honest opinion of that sweater and you didn't ask for it..."

Startled, Michael lifts his right arm and examines the heather-gray material of the sweater's sleeve. "You don't like this sweater?"

"No. It's great. I was just using it as an example. But if I really didn't like it, and I just told you I didn't like it even if you hadn't asked me if I'd liked it or not, well, then, you know...that would kinda be, you know, like how I was when I first started..." The last time she felt this stupid and nervous she'd been stumbling through a toast at her friend Tiffany's wedding, a toast Tiffany had asked her to give at the last minute because no one in Tiffany's family was willing to salute her marriage to a groom who was fifteen years older than her and had shown up to the ceremony in a tuxedo-painted T-shirt and khaki shorts with the bulge of his flask visible in the back pocket. Her face feels like it's turned into sandpaper, her throat like she's breathing through a straw, and all this is distracting her from the fact that Michael Brouchard is pulling his sweater off, sleeve by sleeve, reaching up and adjusting the collar of his shirt, making sure the top button is still undone, before looping the sweater over the top of his satchel. Once he's done, he gives Laney a warm smile.

"Is that better?" he asks.

A patch of hard chest is visible now. And then there's that thick, muscular neck, and those forearms, those forearms of total sexual destruction, forearms she'd love to leave handprints on in her efforts to pull him deeper inside of her. The only thing that would make the scene better would be if he were gently sliding a chocolate covered cherry in between her lips and asking if he could rub her feet.

"Better," she says.

"Good," he says, with a smile that almost knocks her on her ass. Has he ever smiled that way with her in class? Has he ever smiled that way with *anyone* in class?

"So this *I'm not allowed to speak my mind* trip you're on," he says. "I'm feeling like these words aren't entirely yours," Michael says.

"My friend Cat kinda contributed."

"I see..."

"Do you?"

"I feel like I'm seeing more of you today than I ever have."

"Yeah, well, it's the first time we've ever talked outside of class. Really earning your paycheck with that deduction, aren't you professor?"

"Okay. A little bite there. I can see what Cat's talking about."

"Oh, that's nothing, Mister Brouchard."

"Michael..."

"Sorry. Michael."

"It's the Rose Scholarship, isn't it?" he asks suddenly, as if he's nervous to put the question so bluntly.

"I'm sorry?"

"The scholarship you're on. It's the Rose Scholarship."

"You've been researching me?"

"Yes," he says. "Yes, I have." Not sort of. Not kind of. He didn't attach qualifiers to it. He didn't apologize for it, either. He simply said, yes, he's been researching her just like she's been researching him; hunting down his Facebook profile to find out how old he was, Googling his full name to find out where he did his undergraduate work—LSU—and if he was also born in New Orleans—he was, and if like her, he had to fight and claw for just about everything good in his life, or if like most of the other students here, privileges galore had been handed to him on a silver platter by several assistants. She hasn't been able to find an answer to the last question, and she wonders if this is the best way to do it. By actually talking to him, rather than tapping keys on her computer late at night while building a fantasy life for him. For *both* of them.

"Yes," she says. "It's the Elizabeth Rose Scholarship."

"Full ride, but you lose it the minute your GPA drops under a three point six."

"That's the one," she answers.

"That scholarship's got something like six hundred applicants every year. That's pretty damn impressive, Miss Foley. Nothing to be ashamed of."

"Who said I was ashamed?"

"Briffel implied you should be. I'm here to say he's wrong. Dead wrong. And a jerk. But like I said, I'm not supposed to call him that."

"And if I'm not supposed to call you Mister Brouchard, then you shouldn't call me Miss Foley."

"My apologies, Laney."

"No more apologies either. You know, unless you do something really shitty."

"Can I buy you a drink?" he asks. It's the first time he's broken eye contact with her since they started this conversation. "A not-shitty drink."

"Like a *drink*-drink?"

"Yes. You're twenty-three, right? I'm sorry…if you're sober, I didn't mean to..."

Yep. He's totally been Googling me. Or Facebooking me. Or whatever I've been doing to him.

"No. I'm not sober. It's just…"

"Or if there's another way you'd like to celebrate."

"Celebrate what?"

"The fact that you got the Rose Scholarship."

"C'mon. It's not like it's the *Rhodes* Scholarship."

"Now you're starting to sound like Jake Briffel."

"Lord. Kill me now."

"Not a chance. All right, fine, so I guess I missed the big blowout you had when you found out you got the scholarship and that's it? No more celebrations for you?"

"There wasn't a blowout. There wasn't *anything,* really."

"Really?"

"No. When I got the news, I made the mistake of telling my dad."

"The *mistake*?"

"He thinks college is a waste of time. And he thought the time I spent trying to get into a good one was also a waste of time. So mostly he looks at me and just sees…a waste of time."

It's one thing to make this kind of joke with someone like her friend Cat. Sarcasm is their preferred means of communication, after all. But Michael's been so gentle and kind, stating the cold hard fact of her family situation plainly feels like she's showing him an open wound.

"I have a feeling you're a lot more than that," Michael says softly.

"Than a waste of time?" she asks.

"I can't imagine referring to someone of your accomplishments and intelligence as a…waste of time," Michael says. She can feel the pulse of protective anger moving through her teacher as he struggles with these final words, as potent and shiver-inducing as when he stared down that loudmouth Jake Briffel. And because Michael is a polite and intelligent man, she realizes this is his most diplomatic way of calling her father a jackass. Which is exactly what her father is.

"He got over it. Eventually. The way he gets over everything."

"And how's that?"

"He never talks about it again."

"That's rough."

Oh, honey, she almost says. *That's nothing. Let me tell you about the three times I got held up when I was working at the gas station. Or my best friend from high school who dropped out junior year because she got pregnant and ended up turning tricks for six months after she had the kid and before I dragged her into the first rehab that would take her family's crappy health care plan.* But that's the kind of speech Old Laney would have launched into at the drop of a hat, laying it on too thick and too soon so her classmates would know from the get-go she wasn't like them; so she could spare herself the pain of future rejection once they found out where she'd come from.

New Laney lays low. New Laney flies under the radar, blends in as much as she can even though she can't afford the outfits required to do it.

She didn't come to Chamberland University to make friends. She's here because she wants options, the option to be something other than a gas station attendant or a lunch lady. Maybe it *was* her fault she'd never found a way to say that to her father without making him feel bad about his own life. But that's just the way it is. For now, anyway. Until she can get a job good enough that her dad can finally retire. Maybe then he can finally take the time he needs to grieve the loss of her mother, a task he's been putting off for years. But until that blessed time comes, she doesn't want to spend the next three years completely alone as she builds a better life for herself, and while she's got no plans to pledge a sorority any time soon, maybe if she follows Cat's instructions, she'll have less trouble finding study partners.

"It was my fault," she says, because it sounds like something New Laney should say. Humble, meek, obedient. Not angry. Not wounded. Not poor.

"How's that?" Michael asks.

"He'd just worked a double offshore and I shouldn't have—you know, I shouldn't have expected him to be excited for me when he already told me he wouldn't be. I just thought that when the actual news came in, maybe he'd…"

"So what you're saying is you never had a party or a dinner or any kind of celebration at all?"

For some reason, this admission shames her, even though it shouldn't. Even though she wasn't the one who stormed out of the house in a rage because she'd dared to speculate about more than one possible future for herself. But there's no judgment in Michael's voice. There isn't any in his expression either.

"No," she finally says. "Never."

"All right, then. I'll pick you up at seven."

"What?"

"Eight's better? Maybe six thirty?"

"Seven's fine, but what do you—I mean, what are we doing?"

"Where do you live?"

"I'm in Berry Hall on East Campus."

"Great. I'll be outside at seven."

He's walking away quickly.

She calls after him, and when he stops and turns, she can see the eagerness and the fear in his expression, both of which he was trying to hide with a rapid-fire invitation and a hasty escape. A dozen different versions of a rejection gather in her mind. *You're my teacher, I can't. It's not appropriate. You're way too hot. I can't be trusted alone with you.*

"Why don't I meet you there?" she says.

There's a flicker of disappointment in his expression, but his furrowed brow is soon joined by a cocky grin. "But you don't know where we're going," he says.

"Right. That's why you have to tell me."

Don't ask me why. Please don't ask me why I'm afraid to get in a car alone with you. New Laney isn't supposed to tell those kinds of stories anymore.

"Do you know where Perry's is? In the Quarter?"

Everyone knows where Perry's is. It's one of the most famous restaurants in town. All she can manage is a nod.

"See you there at seven, Miss Foley."

His sudden reversion to the use of her last name stabs her in the gut. Is it because she just refused his offer of a ride? Is he rounding down their plans from date to friendly dinner?

A friendly dinner at *Perry's*? Fat chance. A candlelit courtyard, a bubbling fountain, those weathered, fern-dappled French Quarter walls rising on all sides of them. She's seen pictures of the place online and in magazines and it practically oozes romance. If he'd wanted a friendly dinner, there were plenty of diners near campus where they could meet.

"What should I wear?" she calls after him.

"Whatever you like to celebrate in," he says, and then he's disappeared into a crowd of students heading toward the nearby parking lot, and she doesn't manage a deep breath until several minutes after she can't see him anymore.

2

"Either you get some teacher dick tonight or I quit being friends with you."

"Cat! *Honestly*!"

They're heading away from campus and in the direction of the French Quarter when Laney's best friend powers down the driver's side window of her BMW. A brisk wind rips through the leather-upholstered car, blowing Cat Burke's platinum blonde hair back from one side of her angelic face and carrying with it the clatter of the lumbering St. Charles Avenue streetcars they're flying past at Laney doesn't-want-to-know-how-many miles an hour.

Cat drives like she consumes Diet Coke—relentlessly and without regard for her well-being, and Laney knows full well her best friend isn't willing to hear anyone's opinion about either compulsion, including Laney's. But she's startled Cat waited this long to open her window. She usually drives with it down, just like a smoker would. Only Cat isn't a smoker. To Laney's knowledge Cat's never smoked at all, except maybe the occasional joint at a party, after which she usually complains of nausea and heads straight back to her dorm room to take a three-hour nap covered in Funyuns dust. The way Laney figures it, keeping the window open while she drives is one of Cat's many desperate methods for regulating her own body temperature, which always seems to run several degrees above normal, another side effect of being one of the most hyperactive people Laney has ever met.

Cat Burke is always hot. Cat Burke is always full of opinions. Cat Burke always has a plan, usually a plan for someone else. Usually whoever is trapped in her car with her, and usually that person is Laney. And the reason it's taken Cat this long to lower her window is because she's convinced the lecture she's been giving Laney is super-important.

"Cat. Honey. Let's get something clear. You're picking me up tonight even if I don't sleep with him."

"Nope. You'll get a cab. This is an ultimatum, Sister Mary Laney Foley. Like one of those thrillers you love to read when you're in a crappy mood. I'm calling it *The Laney Ultimatum.* Starring Laney, Professor Forearms, and his headboard. See, I know big words too."

"*Forearms* is not a big word."

"I meant *ultimatum*, smart ass!"

"Right, and I get that you *think* it's an ultimatum, Cat. And I think it's sweet that you think you can give me ultimatums. But if you don't pick me up tonight when I call you, I'm going to start a rumor that you're a serial killer. And I'm going to start it on the *WWL Eyewitness News.* Got it?"

"Whatever, Miss Independent," Cat fires back. "You took my ultimatum about the dress, didn't you?"

"I added a jacket."

"After I told you to!" Cat barked.

"You told me to go sleeveless and I refused."

"You're covering up too much 'cause you're trying to pretend like you don't want to sleep with him!"

"I'm trying not to freeze to death!"

"It's sixty-five degrees outside!" Cat whined. "Whatever! For the last time, I am *not* picking you up tonight. And the reason I'm not picking you up tonight is because you are going home with this man the minute he even hints that he wants you to. And you know why?" Cat bends toward her over the gearshift, growling like an angry lion. "Because he's *hhhhhhawwwwwwwwwwt.* With five h's and ten w's."

"And you're being shallow," Laney hissed back, "with twenty s's and eleven o's."

"Oh, don't you get all high and mighty on me. You've been mooning over this guy for months."

"Yeah, and *mooning* isn't necessarily the best basis for a good relationship."

"I'm not talking about *that* kind of mooning!"

"I know what kind of mooning you're talking about. Stop interrupting me! What I'm saying is that *mooning* is something you do over One Direction or Five Seconds of—"

"Oh, so now you're saying you wouldn't go out on a date with One Direction? That's just crazy talk!"

"*The whole band?*"Laney snapped. "Are you nuts? You think I'm just going to lie back and let them take turns?"

"I guess that sounds better in the fanfic version," Cat muttered.

"What kind of fanfic are you reading?"

"Leave me alone. Tumblr doesn't do it for me."

"Cat, let's just agree that you and I have different value systems in this area, okay?"

"Oh, kiss my butt, Laney Foley. Kiss my *butt* with your value systems!"

"I don't even know what that means."

"You have been making goo-goo eyes at Michael Brouchard for the whole semester and now he finally got the message and suddenly you're a nun? Oh, and by the way, the guy's not only *hot* but he likes to talk about the kinda stuff you like to talk about and—"

"And what kind of *stuff* is that?"

"Oh, you know," Cat answers, talking under her breath and out of one corner of her mouth. "Art and books. And—more art."

"Why are we friends?"

"'Cause I don't put up with your b.s., girlfriend. Day one, I saw right through your whole routine."

"I don't have a routine," Laney groans, even though she does. Or she did, and she knows Cat's right.

"Hi, I'm Laney," Cat's impersonation captures the quiet tone Laney often drops into her voice because it softens the harsh Cajun accent she inherited from her mother. "And I can never enjoy life or have any fun because I have to work harder than you because my parents didn't buy me a car—"

"They *didn't* buy me a car. They have *never* bought me a car, and they never will buy me a car, Miss BMW, because they can barely afford to buy themselves a car."

"Be that as it may!" Cat responds with the grand dismissiveness of an inconvenienced monarch. "You still act like you have to work harder than me—"

"I *do* have to work harder than you," Laney says. "If my GPA drops below a three point six, I don't get to go to school here anymore. If you get a C, your father sends you consolation roses."

"*Be* that as it *may,*" Cat responds with a careful and menacing enunciation that tells Laney's she's on the verge of pointing out one too many hard facts about their vastly different backgrounds. "When you're not working, it's your responsibility to actually enjoy your life. And that does not include staying in your dorm room all night reading sad books about gnomes."

"There are no *gnomes* in *Lord of the Rings*."

"Still!"

"And the trilogy has a happy ending, by the way."

"Says you."

"And you know, there are some people who consider Tolkien to be one of the greatest novelists of all time."

"And if he could get you to go outside once in a while, I'd feel the same."

"Seriously. Why are we friends?"

"'Cause I'm one of the only people you couldn't scare away when you got here," Cat says. There's more truth to that statement than Laney would like. "So don't you scare him away tonight just because he makes you have feelings you can't control. That's all I'm saying, okay?"

Despite the degree to which the woman frays her nerves, Laney adores Cat Burke. Her new best friend shares the loud, brassy no-time-for-bullshit quality of some of Laney's favorite cousins, and her dad on a good day, and that's the real reason they became friends right off the bat. Most of the other girls at school were too busy finding eight hundred different ways to avoid expressing a real feeling that might endanger their chances of landing a rich husband. But Laney's favorite thing about Cat by far is her tendency to cap off an elaborate diatribe with the expression, *That's all I'm saying, okay?*

They ride in silence for a few minutes, a silence punctuated by Cat's desperate slurps from her Diet Coke.

"This is a risk," Laney finally says. "This is a really big risk, Cat."

"Most good things are, honey."

"Still."

"Still what?"

"He's…"

"Three years older than you. That's all. Who cares what the rule book says?"

"I care what my scholarship says," Laney says. She's staring out the window at the passing parade of Greek Revival mansions, houses she used to dream of living in as a child, never once believing she'd someday have the chance to attend college in the same neighborhood.

"You're really afraid he's going to drop your grade if you have one bad date?" Cat asks softly, as if she can sense the thoughts running through Laney's head won't be dispelled by a smart remark or a sarcastic ultimatum.

"No," Laney says. "No, of course not. I'm afraid we're gonna have one really good date. *Really* good. And then another really good date. And then another. And then something will…"

"Something will what?" Cat asks. The bite and the fight have both gone out of her voice.

"Something will go wrong. I don't know. He'll lose interest. Or maybe I will. Maybe he'll turn out to…"

Maybe he'll pin me to the passenger seat by throwing one strong arm across my chest like Bobby Dautrieve did, start snarling at me about how I'm a bitch and a tease cause all I wanted to do was kiss, and who the hell did I think I was trying to get myself into a good school when really I'd never do better than a good-looking guy like him. And maybe then, I won't have my father's switchblade like I did with Bobby, won't have the wherewithal to drive it down in between his legs, close enough to snag the fabric of his jeans on the blade, but not his flesh. Won't have the time to get away like I did with Bobby, 'cause he wasn't sure if he'd been stabbed or not so he just decided to scream his head off while I ran fast enough to beat the band.

"Laney?" Cat's voice cuts through the scary flashback strobing through Laney's mind.

"Maybe he'll turn out to be horrible and then I'll feel like I'm stuck with him 'til the semester's over. Just so he won't punish me."

"He won't punish you, Laney."

"You don't know that. *I* don't know that. *He* probably doesn't even know that. Jerks never think they're jerks."

"Exactly. Bad men don't wear uniforms. But the good ones don't either. That's why you gotta see what they've got under their clothes to find out who they *really* are. You know what I'm saying?"

"I know you're talking about sex. Again."

"No, I'm using sex to point out what Professor Forearms would probably call a *universal truth*."

"Now that is a pretty big word. Or term, excuse me."

"Uh-huh. Whatever. Point is, if you're going to find out who someone is, you actually have to get to know them. And sometimes that means taking a risk."

"I know that. But this is a *big* risk, Cat."

"Right. And maybe that means it'll be a big reward."

"You know, you act like you're this big sex bomb, but it's not like you're hopping into beds all over campus or anything."

"Laney, I'm not talking about the size of his junk. I'm talking about *life*."

"Life?"

"Yeah. *Life*. You can't live life in your head or in books. And you can't live it in fear either."

"I know. I just—"

"Just *nothing*. You deserve something better than fending off drunken frat boys. For one, you're older than most of them, and for two, you don't have much in common with any of them. *This* guy might be just right for you."

"This *teacher*," she says. "This teacher might be just right for me."

"Whatever. If he does anything remotely shitty I'll totally lie to everyone and say he put his hands all over me and tried to trade grades for sex."

"You're not one of his students."

"Who cares? I'll get one of his actual students to do it. I'm real persuasive with Jell-O shots."

The image of Cat and one of Laney's stumbling, inebriated classmates trying to recount a badly rehearsed and bogus tale of sexual harassment to a school administrator reduces Laney to tears of laughter.

"Or you could just agree to pick me up tonight," Laney says. "That would make things a lot easier. For now, at least."

"Oh, of course, I will. You don't really think I'm going to leave you stranded down there if it doesn't go well?"

"I don't know. You can be pretty stubborn, Cat."

"Takes one to know one," Cat says. "No, seriously. I'll pick you up if you need me to. That said, a real gentleman would drive you home even if he ain't gettin' any. Info like that is all part of the discovery process."

"Yeah, well, I don't get in cars with guys on the first date."

"Yet another thing you're gonna have to get over."

Laney ponders telling Cat the story of Bobby Dautrieve and her father's switchblade, but she's in no mood to let any of her horrible past dating experiences out of the little boxes she keeps them in, not when she's poised to have a night so magical it could make them all seem like hazy, distant memories.

"One thing at a time, Cat," Laney answers, before she realizes she's squeezing her clasped hands in between her knees tightly enough to cause pain in the heels of both palms. "One thing at a time."

3

Laney has walked past Perry's countless times during French Quarter bar crawls, gazing covetously into its lantern-lit courtyard. She's always assumed the only way she'd be able to score a meal there would be if a friend of hers landed a job as a bartender. But now, here she is, giving Michael's last name to the restaurant's handsome maître d', following him under a soaring wrought iron archway that feels like the gateway to a royal palace.

Most of the restaurant is contained inside a restored, two-story carriage house that sits at the back of an expansive, planter-filled courtyard. The house has a long, narrow balcony traveling the length of its second floor, and at one corner of it, Michael stands behind his empty chair next to a candlelit table for two. Laney's got at least another minute of following the host through the rings of cast iron tables that surround the courtyard's gurgling stone fountain before she reaches him, but her teacher has already greeted her arrival like a perfect gentleman.

Once inside, Laney mounts the rickety wooden steps leading to the second floor, her heart hammering the whole time. Her outfit is a fail, she's suddenly sure of it. She should have listened to Cat. And she's frantically re-dressing Michael in her mind, making him less imposing, less dashing, less desirable. But when she steps out onto the balcony, he looks even better than he did from below. His brown corduroy blazer has leather elbow patches, and the top three buttons of his dark blue dress shirt are undone. When she's within a few feet of the table, she catches a whiff of his cologne, an intoxicating scent that makes her think of backyard campfires and vanilla ice cream. Then she sees the Mylar balloons tied to the back of her empty chair, stamped with celebratory expressions written in various bright colors: CONGRATULATIONS!

AMAZING! GOOD WORK!

Michael Brouchard has staged the congratulatory dinner she never had, the one her father effectively canceled a year before when he stormed out of the house in a rage. As if the balloons weren't enough, there's a bottle of champagne chilling in an ice bucket next to the table. Laney hesitates behind her empty chair, grasping the back of it with one sweaty hand. She reads the champagne bottle's label in the flickering candlelight. It's Veuve Clicquot, the vintage, her first year of high school.

They've only had one conversation that's lasted longer than a few minutes, and already Michael has filled a gap in her life. Not only that, he recognized it was there in the first place, that it was pulling at the fabric of her self-worth more than she wanted to admit. She knew tonight would be full of seductive risks, but didn't expect to start here, with an overwhelming sense of having been seen and heard and valued.

He gestures to her empty chair, waits for her to take her seat before taking his own. Only once she's seated does she realize Michael had extended his hand toward hers and she'd been too distracted by the balloons and the champagne to notice. Now there's no going back to rectify her rudeness without sounding like a sputtering idiot. The host, who has stood by politely throughout her hesitation, hands her a menu and departs. She's folding her napkin across her lap when she sees a large envelope resting against the edge of her plate, as large as a wedding invite. Her name is written on the outside in precise, draftsman-like handwriting. Just her first name. Not her last name. And not *Miss Foley,* which they both agreed he wouldn't call her anymore.

Laney.

Her hands shake as she tears open the envelope, as she unfolds the piece of heavy sketch paper inside of it. The breath goes out of her when she finds herself staring down at the amazingly detailed pencil sketch of—*me. That's* me. *That's me holding a rose in one hand while more rose petals shower down all sides of me. Roses for the Rose Scholarship. Oh, my God. He* drew *me.*

The card seems to waver suddenly. She's blinking back tears.

She can't remember the last time anyone has been this thoughtful, this kind. She's never thought of herself as a victim of abuse. But what do you call an entire lifetime of having your own intelligence, your own competence used against you, an entire lifetime of everyone from your parents to your friends thinking they don't really have to show up for you because you do such a good job of showing up for yourself?

Sometimes you don't know you've got a shell around your heart until it cracks.

Get it together, Laney. Get it—

"Laney…are you all right?" Michael asks.

A sane and reasonable answer is right on the tip of her tongue.

And then she snorts.

Her hand flies to her nose to prevent a messy disaster, but there's no hiding the tears now. And Michael's expression goes from slightly wounded—maybe he thought she was about to laugh at all his beautiful gestures—to outright concern.

"Wow," Michael mutters. "I better cancel the violinist."

"Michael…"

"I know. I said I was just going to buy you a drink and I kinda—"

"Michael, I can't. This is …"

"This is what?"

"You're my teacher," she whispers.

Even in the candlelight, she can see his cheeks reddening. The last thing she wanted to do was embarrass him, and God knows the last thing she wanted to do was cry.

"Has nobody ever done anything nice for you, Laney?"

She goes rigid, feels herself reaching for the same kind of smart comeback she'd use if Cat hit her with the same accusatory question.

"This isn't just nice," she says.

"Good," he says, staring into her eyes, "because I didn't do it just to be *nice*."

The lust in his tone brings a flush of heat to the sides of her neck, to the spot between her shoulder blades that always gets tingly when he looks at her, to the insides of her thighs. It paints gooseflesh down her arms. And by the time she's done savoring this light suggestion of his desire for her, her tears have dried and her throat feels clear again.

"The card was too much," he says quickly. "I'm sorry."

"No, it wasn't," she responds. "Please. Don't be sorry."

"No. Maybe I should have drawn something else. Something that had meaning, but wasn't…you know, *you*. It's just… Well, when I got home this afternoon, I was trying to remember the artists you liked so I could use something from one of their works. But I kept remembering the way you looked when we said good-bye and I—"

"You drew it this *afternoon*?" she asks, dumbfounded, waving the card in the air next to her. She knew he was a scholar, but she didn't know he was also an artist himself.

"Yeah, I know. Too much."

"It's not too much," she says, taking care to fold up the card, return it to its envelope and slide it into her purse. It's the least she can do after treating it like a handkerchief.

"Is it a *little* too much?" he asks.

He makes a small space between the thumb and index finger on his right hand, and that's when she can see from his cocked eyebrow and the slight dimple in his chin, that he's being a *little* sarcastic. He doesn't regret a thing he's done, despite how they've done her in. The balloons, the champagne, the card; he wouldn't take any of them back for an instant.

"It isn't too much," she says.

"I know," he says quietly.

"But it's dangerous."

"Dangerous," he says, as if it's the first time he's heard the word.

"That thing I said earlier. About you being my teacher. That's still true."

"I know," he says. "And I like that you keep pointing that out."

"Why?"

"Because it means you want me as much as I want you," he says.

"How do you figure that?"

"People don't point out barriers unless they want to overcome them."

"Yeah, and that can be a dangerous thing," she counters.

"If it's not done right, maybe."

"Anyway we do it might be dangerous, Michael."

"What kind of man do you think I am?" he asks with a mischievous smile, far more mischievous than any he's given her, or anyone, for that matter, in class.

"I don't know. *Yet.*"

"Well, that's why we're here, then," he says. "This is why dates were invented. Even if they start off kinda weird."

"So this is a date?" she asks.

"Please tell me you didn't think otherwise."

She laughs against her will, and he bites his bottom lip gently at the sound of it, his eyes brightening and the angel's press under his nose becoming more pronounced as he suppressed a grin.

"Okay," she says. "It's a date."

"Good. How else would I get to hear you say the word *dangerous* over and over again like it's a dessert you've been craving all day?"

"You didn't really hire a violinist, did you?"

"No."

"Good, you know, 'cause all of this is…good enough. It's *way* good enough."

"I hired a mariachi band for later. You know, to walk us down Bourbon Street."

As she barks with laughter, she feels her hand start a quick trip toward her blushing neck. She wills it to her lap, closes her left hand over it.

"Brass bands are so overdone, you know?" he says.

"Uh-huh."

He hasn't opened the champagne bottle yet. She's not about to ask him too, not after her mini-breakdown. But she could really use a glass or two or three or four.

Just then, the handsome waiter appears and rattles off a bunch of specials she doesn't hear because she's too busy watching Michael watch the waiter with an intense set to his jaw. It's like he's using the waiter's arrival to catch his breath after the tension and awkwardness of the last few minutes. And just this slight evidence of emotional strain on his face calms her slightly. But only slightly.

Despite his handsomeness, and despite his heartwarming gifts and the effort—and cash—he put into them, she can't stop seeing him as a luxury she can't afford. And she fears that no matter what he says, no matter what he does, nothing will stop the march of anxiety and doubt across her mind.

Maybe it never stops, she thinks suddenly, in a voice so clear it seems almost divine. *Maybe the doubts and the fears never go away. Maybe you just take the risk anyway and see what happens because what happens might be wonderful. And maybe the risk is easier to take once he embraces you, once his breath is against your neck.*

She's gotten so lost in thought she's startled to find them alone again.

"Hear anything you like?" he asks.

"To be honest, I wasn't really paying attention."

"Me neither."

"What? Seriously? You looked like you were hanging on his every word."

"I wasn't."

"You had me fooled."

"Good, I guess. I mean, I didn't ask you here to *fool* you. But hey, if we ever play poker."

Don't make a joke about strip poker. Please don't make a creepy joke about strip poker.

After a few minutes of Michael not making a joke about strip poker, Laney finally becomes convinced he's not going to make a joke about strip poker.

"Strip poker!" Michael barks.

When she realizes he read her mind throughout their long silence, she rocks forward, hands to her mouth, to keep her laughter from seizing control of her entire body.

Michael is undeterred; he makes *ooga-boogah* motions with both hands in the air in front of him. "*Stripping…nudity reference…first date…awwwwwkward,*" he continues like he's narrating the trailer for a 1950's horror film.

"Stop," she begs in-between gasps.

"*Awkwaaaaard,*" he adds one last time, in a softer version of his full-throated Vincent Price impersonation. He punctuates it with two fluttery hand motions, then he sits back in his chair, bright-eyed and beaming because his joke hit home.

It takes her a while to get her breath back. She's run such a gamut of emotions in such a short time, she feels exhausted to the point of near delirium. She wishes she could bottle this moment, this easy, if a little breathless, smile they're sharing now. At the very least, she wants to fix it in place and keep the rest of the date somewhere in its vicinity. God knows, they've already wandered far from the evening she'd scripted for them both before she arrived; polite flirting followed by a gentle give-and-take of not-too-personal personal details, all of it building up to the reveal, on both of their parts, of some sort of personal trauma in their respective pasts. (This final act, she had hoped, would be accompanied by copious amounts of booze.)

But he's sidelined her by giving her something she didn't realize had been taken from her, some celebration of the fact she landed an impossible-to-get scholarship. As a result, she's made known the depth of her attraction to him against her will. Now that he's read her mind as well—*strip poker!*—and made her laugh until she thought she was going to pass out, what choice do they have left except for total candor, total honesty?

"We could always wait," Laney says.

"For what? I wasn't exactly planning to throw you across the table right here if that's what you—"

"Until the end of the semester. Until you weren't my teacher anymore."

"So you want to call it a night and try this again in a couple months?" he asks with a wry smile.

"Well, not right now I don't want to call it a night. I mean, I'm kinda hungry."

"Oh, well, good. 'Cause we're at a restaurant."

"I can see that. A restaurant with balloons."

"*I* brought those balloons. The best the restaurant could do was a candle in a piece of bread pudding. That would never do."

"Let's see the night through. If that's okay."

"This night can end however you want it to, Laney Foley."

"Thank you, Michael Brouchard."

"In fact, I'll even let you take that champagne bottle home with you if you'd like. That way you won't be unfairly influenced by a spirit you can't contain. Get it. Spirit. 'Cause it's alcohol?"

"The strip poker thing was funnier."

"Yeah, well, they can't all be winners."

"You're a winner. That's all that counts."

He cocks his head to one side, lifts his glass to toast her. He doesn't milk every compliment she gives him for all it's worth, doesn't press her to elaborate or clarify, and she likes that. So many of the men in her life, including her father, have demanded constant validation from her while pretending never to need it, and sometimes the contradiction makes her head spin. But not with Michael. Not so far, at least.

"I thought about it, you know," Michael says quietly.

"Thought about what?" she asks, startled by the sudden seriousness of his tone.

"Waiting until the semester was over."

"Why didn't you?" she asks.

"I tried waiting once. It didn't go so well."

"What do you mean?"

Michael grips his water glass, brings it to his mouth and takes a thirsty gulp. His eyes have left hers for the first time since the waiter arrived. She can't tell if the memory he's about to impart wounds him to this day, or if he's simply embarrassed by what he's about to reveal.

"I met her my junior year at LSU. She had a boyfriend and I didn't want to do anything to screw up anybody's relationship, so I kept my mouth shut. Then they had some kind of fight or falling out. I couldn't really tell and I thought if I asked too many questions, it would make it obvious that I was into her. So I kept my mouth shut and just tired to be a *good guy friend* and all that. And little by little, I managed to find out she and the guy had separated. He was going off to med school in Houston and she didn't want to leave Louisiana. Anyway, the point is it took me weeks to get all the info because I was all about flying below the radar. Playing it super-safe. I didn't want it getting back to her that I was asking around just in case she and the boyfriend were still serious. Finally I worked up the nerve to ask her out, but a couple weeks turned out to be too long."

"She got back together with the guy?"

"No," he answers, staring down into his water glass, working his jaw slightly as if a piece of gum were stuck to the back of his teeth. "She was listening to her iPod and she stepped off the curb before the light changed and a truck hit her. She died instantly."

"Oh my God," Laney says. It's more of a sharp exhalation than a statement.

"So that's why when a woman walks into my life who has everything you do, I don't wait."

Or you tell her this story, which sounds too good to be true. Or just bad enough that it's too bad to be—

—shut up, *Laney. He's looking you in the eye, for Christ's sake. Liars don't look people straight in the eye.*

"What was her name?"

"Brooke."

Yeah—and her last *name, Nicholas Sparks?*

—Shut up, Laney!

"I'm so sorry, Michael."

"Listen, I didn't tell the story to get a Purple Heart. Honestly, was she the love of my life? I have no idea. But that's the point. I have no idea because I never stepped up to bat. I wasted too much time waiting for the moment to be perfect. I don't want to make the same mistake with you, Laney."

The waiter arrives. Laney isn't remotely ready to order, but she pops open the menu and pretends to study its contents. She can't think of a better way to hide her suspicion the story Michael just shared with her isn't true.

Or maybe only half-true, which would be just as lame.

"Ready?" Michael asks.

"I'll be ready by the time you've ordered," she mutters.

She's not, but she orders anyway. Something not too expensive, something that won't leave her bloated and sleepy.

Once the waiter departs, she bends forward, as if she's about to take Michael into confidence. "Bathroom," she whispers, and then gestures to her face, which she assumes is still tear-splotched.

He smiles and nods.

It's a single bathroom, thank God, and when she throws the lock, her first deep breath in hours fills her lungs. Relief, that's what she's feeling, relief that she might be about to catch Michael in a lie, that she might be on the verge of freeing herself from this whole reckless mess.

If she were able to afford a smartphone of her own, she wouldn't have to stoop to calling Cat. But she can't afford one, so calling Cat it is.

Here goes, she thinks.

Cat answers. "What are you doing?"

"Where are you?"

"Answering questions with questions. Not a good sign."

"I need your help," Laney says.

"Don't tell me he's being weird. Ugh. Is he being weird? I can meet you out front. I'm at CC's."

"Wait, seriously? You're a few blocks away?"

"Yeah," Cat answers.

"What happened to not picking me up if I didn't go home with him?"

"I was *joking*. You really think I'd leave you down here without a car?"

"That's actually really sweet."

As sweet as expensive champagne, balloons and a custom-made hand-drawn card. But she hadn't done the best at accepting those gifts either.

"Laney, *why* are you calling?"

"Do you have wifi?"

"Uhm, yeah. How do you think I'm passing the time?"

"Google something for me."

"Okay. I'm ready," Cat says, without bothering to ask for an explanation.

"Brooke. LSU. Truck. Accident. Killed Instantly."

"What kind of date is this?" Cat asks.

"You're looking for news articles or an obituary from about two or three years ago."

"Oh my God. You're fact-checking your date! Seriously? You're having me *fact-check* your date?"

"If I had a smart phone, I'd do it myself. Now start Googling."

Silence falls on the other end, followed by the click of laptop keys, followed by a few grunts here and there as Cat scans the search results.

"Here it is," Cat finally says. "A news story from three years ago." She quickly skims through the story, "*Baton Rouge Police have announced that alcohol did not play a factor in the accident that killed a Louisiana State University junior three days ago. Twenty-one-year-old art history major Brooke Daniels was struck and killed by a cold storage truck at three in the afternoon while walking home from class. The driver did not flee the scene and has been cooperating with authorities since the accident. The announcement from Baton Rouge P.D. seems to confirm witness reports that Daniels was listening to music on her iPod and appeared distracted when she stepped into the intersection before the light changed…* Do I have to keep reading?"

"No," Laney says. "He was telling the truth."

"So you *were* fact-checking him? Honestly. Laney, no one's going to be able to fall in love with this guy *for* you. Go back to the table!"

Cat hangs up.

Now that it's gone, she's embarrassed by the sense of relief that filled her when she thought Michael might turn out to be a liar. Would it really have been a comfort to know he was just like a dozen other scam artists and players she'd managed to expose before things got serious?

Christ, was she already *that* bitter?

Bitter.

That's probably the least of what Michael would think of her if he knew she hadn't believed his story.

Did he get a whiff of her suspicions? Did she leave the table too quickly?

There's a sparkling champagne flute sitting next to her empty plate, and when she takes her seat again, he gives her a smile as warm as the one he gave her when she first sat down.

"I thought the whole cork-popping thing wouldn't have been appropriate given we kind of started off awkwardly," he says, lifting his glass. "But we can still do this part."

She returns his toast and takes a hearty slug of champagne. Hearty enough to cause Michael's eyes to widen while he takes a polite, restrained sip from his own glass. He sets his glass down with a thud that sounds final. Laney sees the strain behind his smile.

"You didn't believe me, did you?" he asks.

"How'd you know?"

"Your face looks exactly the same. You didn't splash water on it or anything."

CIA, here I come.

"No," she answers. "I didn't believe you."

"And now you do?"

"Yes. I did some research."

"Wow. That's one hell of a bathroom they got here."

"I'm sorry."

Michael stares down into his champagne glass. *Strike two*, she thinks. *One more strike and you're—*

"So I guess a lot of guys have lied to you on first dates before," he says with a lack of anger that surprises her.

"Yes, but still…"

"Okay. Let me just say a few things."

"I'm listening," she answers, trying not to sound too relieved that she's temporarily off the hook for explaining her suspicions.

"You need to learn that *cannot* is not two words."

"What?"

"Also, I encourage you to get a copy of *The Elements of Style* by Strunk and White and read the section on paragraphs, because sometimes you cram what should be about three paragraphs into one and it can make your papers confusing."

"You're talking about my classwork? Right now?"

"Yes."

"I wasn't aware it was a class in composition."

"If you didn't have any talent for analyzing and discussing art, I wouldn't be worried about your composition. But you do, so I am. Also, I know you're a bigger fan of periods like Baroque and Rococo, but you're going to have to stop leaving out *all* Renaissance painters when we do comparison assignments. Because whether or not their work appeals to you on a personal level, we can't just ignore the entire Renaissance when we survey trends in Western Art that started in the Middle Ages."

"I see…"

"Do you?"

"Yeah, you're attacking me because I didn't believe your story."

"No, Laney. I'm proving to you that no matter what happens between us, I'll still be able to do my job. At the end of the semester, you'll get the grade you deserve, based on the work you've done in class. Not based on whether you let me do the things to your body I've wanted to do now for months."

What things? Tell me now. All of them. Each and every one. Tell me what you want to do to my—

"I have a copy of Strunk and White," she says, downing a shot of champagne.

"As we all should."

"It doesn't exactly make for sexy bedtime reading."

"You don't strike me as the type who reads a lot of romance novels."

"*You* strike me as the type who does. For strategy."

"A woman who can't handle criticism. I can handle that."

"Excuse me?"

Michael bows his head and holds up his palms in a gesture of defeat.

"That was shitty," he says. "I'm sorry."

The sincerity of his apology dissolves the anger that's been blocking her own. "I'm sorry I didn't believe your story."

"I'm sorry so many guys have lied to you in the past."

Before either of them can be sorry for anything else, like the weather, perhaps, or the fact that humankind has yet to invent a flying car, the waiter brings their food. Once he departs, she realizes this is the moment when she should tell a story of her own, a revelation that could make up for her suspicions of his own, something that balances the scales, make her as vulnerable as he made himself.

I'm already vulnerable, she thinks. And there it is, that hard knot of resistance that won't seem to fade no matter what she does. No matter what *he* does.

"I read a romance novel once," she finally says.

"*Pride and Prejudice*?"

"No! It was contemporary. I can't remember the name. It was *sweet*."

"You say that like it's a bad thing."

"Contemporary?" she asks, teasing him.

"No," he answers with a smile. "Sweet."

"Sweet's all right, I guess."

"But you're not a fan of happily ever after?"

"Sure. If, you know, it's *earned*."

"Earned? How?" he asks, eyes wide as he takes a large bite of food, a sign that he won't be rushing to fill the silence if she doesn't answer because he'll be too busy chewing.

"I don't know yet."

He chews and chews and *chews.*

"Want to learn?" he asks.

"I'll answer after you swallow that bite."

He makes a show of swallowing his bite.

"Well…want to?"

"We'll see," she says.

He shoots her a wicked grin, and when he attacks his plate again with a fork and a knife, she imagines it's with the same force and passion he'd like to unleash on her body.

This night can end however you'd like it to, Laney Foley.

Isn't that how he put it?

She hopes he's a man of his word because the only thing she's sure of is the night's not over yet.

4

LILLIANE

Lilliane Williams isn't afraid to walk the French Quarter alone at night, even in a black leather dress that flatters her curves, even while carrying a jeweled leather suitcase so shiny and ornate it could make the steeliest pickpocket salivate with desire. She doesn't hesitate to cut through back alleys. She takes her time strolling lonely, shadowy side streets. Her primary concern isn't assault; it's encountering someone who might realize she hasn't aged a day in fifty-six years.

But if she were to run into someone from her old life, her life before she wandered into that strange candle shop in April of 1959, that person would probably assume she was a distant relative of Lilliane Williams. Maybe even a reincarnated version. But not the same woman who worked as a housekeeper for a wealthy white family in the Garden District for several years, the same Lilliane Williams whose disappearance wasn't even reported by the local papers because back then the local papers didn't report on the disappearances of black people.

When she's several feet from the opening of an alley, Lilliane senses the low, quick approach of a stalking human predator, hears something behind her that could either be the cock of a gun or the click of a switchblade. As soon as the man grabs for the suitcase, she wills him headfirst into the nearest stone wall. But whatever drugs are coursing through his system have made him impervious to solid concrete and oblivious to her show of supernatural strength.

He whirls, gun raised.

"Lord! *Really?*" she says with a groan.

"Give it to me, bitch, or I'll fucking put a bullet in you. Swear to God."

"If you insist," Lilliane answers brightly.

She sets the suitcase down on the pavement in front of her. Then, just as the thief goes for the handle, she stretches her arms out on either side of her and rises twenty feet straight up into the air, tendrils of gold dust spraying from her open palms like two small bursts of heavenly rocket exhaust. Her miraculous self-propulsion flattens the flaps of her leather dress around her legs with a sound like giant wings beating the air. Perhaps it's reckless to perform this trick right here, right now; just beyond the neon-lit mouth of the alley is a parade of tourists. But this display of power is working its intended effect on her would-be attacker.

The shower of gold dust coats the suitcase, causing the guy to recoil in horror, and the sight of her rising into the air literally knocks him onto his ass. When Lilliane sees his gun spinning across the pavement away from him, she allows herself to sink back down to earth, but not before landing one swift kick to the young man's jaw.

"Run along now, little boy. I've got a date."

Reeking of fresh urine, he does as instructed.

Lilliane picks up the suitcase and continues on her way.

A date? *Not really.*

More like a regular delivery. Sure, it sounds dry, far too mechanical to describe the miraculous contents of the suitcase she's once again carrying confidently in one hand. But while the man scheduled to appear to her in twenty minutes' time is most certainly handsome, there's very little between them she'd be willing to call affection. So she shouldn't call it a date, just as she shouldn't call Bastian Drake a *man.*

What an absurd name, she thinks. She's fairly sure it's not even his real one. But over the years Bastian, or whoever he is, has remained as closely guarded with the details of his own history as he was on that summer afternoon in 1959 when they met for the first time. Despite all their fights, he's never once revealed what his life was like before he took that ridiculous name, before he became the candlemaker, before he became a… Silly that even now her mind trips over the exact word for him, as if just thinking it to herself amounts to some kind of confession.

Ghost. Bastian is a ghost.

Her plight is easier to manage when she's angry, and there are other descriptions of him she prefers because they allow her to remain in a state of barely controlled, but energizing rage.

Captor, owner, overseer, warlock. If he had told me that day what his candle could really do. If he had told me what the consequences would be if I didn't—

A few steps into Jackson Square, she slams into a pedestrian, some drunken little white boy whose wide eyes fill immediately with lustful admiration at the sight of the gorgeous, full-figured black woman in the form-fitting leather dress. She can't lie to herself; she appreciates the attention, feels a deep, growling urge to take him to the nearest alley, strip him of his clothes, place her hands against his blushing, sweating cheeks and stare right into his soul. But she has made a commitment to use her powers in only the most secret and structured way, and only on the willing. That's why she built The Desire Exchange. And performing a radiance on a fresh-faced college boy in the middle of the French Quarter on a Friday night is far more reckless than the aerial routine she just pulled on her would-be mugger.

Those eyes, though. That sweet boyish face…

The skinny little blonde who suddenly hooks the guy under one armpit must be his girlfriend. How else to explain her sudden possessiveness and the dagger-glare she gives Lilliane as she drags Lilliane's not-so-secret admirer off into the crowd?

As she watches the not-so-happy couple disappear, sadness blooms inside of Lilliane like ink meeting water. Sadness tinged with grief. Maybe they're truly in love. Maybe later that night they will fight and scream and cry and then tearfully make up, their feelings for each other renewing, strengthening before exploding into a crescendo of fiery make-up sex. These things have all been lost to Lilliane, thanks to Bastian Drake.

Well, not the sex. She can manage the sex just fine. Better than ever, in fact. It's amazing how skilled you can become in the bedroom when you have all the time in the world to study the act of lovemaking and you suffer none of the costs of aging.

But all the feelings humans tangle throughout the bedroom and beyond, all the emotions humans call *love*, those are gone now. They've been gone for decades.

Lilliane pauses to catch her breath, to flush the poison of grief and regret from her system. She studies the tarot card readers, the street musicians, and the knots of drunken tourists. The brightly lit facade of St. Louis Cathedral rises overhead.

She loves the French Quarter. Unlike many of her fellow radiants, she doesn't leave the compound very often, but when she does, it's to come here. She doesn't have to work to blend in because in the French Quarter, all you have to do to blend in is dance with the chaos. Still, what must the people all around her assume she must be? A cocktail waitress, a street performer, or God forbid, a stripper?

If they find her outfit strange, they'd find the real explanation for it even stranger. The leather dress is perfectly weighted to provide just enough drag to keep her on target when she takes to the air. Radiants can't fly; they leap, and if they don't posses the muscle-strength, or if they haven't weighted themselves down properly, a leap can turn into something that looks like a zigzagging balloon after the air's been let out of it.

Suitcase in hand, Lilliane heads down Pirate's Alley and into a long pool of shadows that rises up the cathedral's side wall. She gives a quick glance in both directions. Confident she's alone, she rises skyward until she's crested one of the flat areas of the roof that sits on either side of the cathedral's spire.

5

"Beautiful, isn't it?" These words are the first sounds Bastian makes as he materializes on the roof of St. Louis Cathedral. No doubt he's referring to the expansive view. Lilliane studies the vast shadowed square below.

At night, the high wrought iron gates, which usually grant admittance to the center of Jackson Square, are closed, leaving the proud statue of Andrew Jackson astride his horse alone in a sea of shadows. Outside the fence, the tarot card readers and street musicians she stood among only seconds before look like small, animated dolls. And just beyond the stream of traffic on Decatur Street, a cargo ship as tall as a high-rise office building glides past the city on the inky black waters of the Mississippi River.

"And to think, most will never see it," Bastian says.

"See what?"

"The *view*, darling. It's not like there's a viewing platform up here."

"Don't attempt to mollify me with talk of my powers," Lilliane says quietly. "I'm not in the mood, Bastian."

"*Mollify* you?" he asks, sounding genuinely hurt. "What a curious word."

She hands him the suitcase with enough force to knock a normal man back on his heels. But he is not a normal man. *At what point are you allowed to stop referring to a ghost as a* man?

Bastian is suddenly silent as he hefts the suitcase. He goes about his usual routine; caressing the handle slowly, carefully running his fingers along the array of inset jewels along the top. To a curious onlooker he would look like some kind of leather fetishist. The truth is far stranger. Bastian cannot slip through the cracks in human time carrying any object he hasn't handled for at least ten minutes. It's one of the few rules of his existence he's shared with her.

"Yes, it's lighter than usual," she says after the silence between them becomes uncomfortable. She had expected him to mention it first.

"And your mood?"

"Normally, I bring you six jars. This time I've got two. You'll make do, I'm sure."

"Your *mood*, Lilliane. What's troubling you this evening?"

"I normally seem pleasant during our little visits?"

"Perhaps not," Bastian answers, nonplussed as always. "But you rarely say anything as specific as *I'm in a bad mood.* So I thought I might take a chance and ask."

"I didn't say I was in a *bad* mood. I said I wasn't in the mood to be distracted with talk of my abilities."

"Distracted from what?"

"None of your business."

"I see."

She could leap from the roof in an instant, ending this awkward little exchange. Bastian would have to stay right where he was. Unlike her, he doesn't have the power to leap tall buildings in a single bound, and unlike him, she doesn't have the power to simply vanish at will. But Bastian won't go anywhere until he's made enough physical contact with the suitcase to spirit it away. Away to wherever it is he goes; she knows better than to ask him exactly where.

"There was a boy," she says. "Down there somewhere."

"A boy?"

"A college kid. In the square, just now. He gave me a look. A look that made me remember things. Things I miss."

"I see."

"Somehow I doubt that," she says quietly.

"And someday, sooner than he thinks, that boy will be a man. Paunchy and middle-aged and stewing in regret over the roads not taken, and you will still be Lilliane. Youthful and powerful and capable of bringing a person's innermost desires to life."

"I tired of these conversations years ago."

"*Two* jars," he says.

"Managerial difficulties. Don't trouble yourself."

"Consider me troubled. I helped you build The Desire Exchange, Lilliane. And I did it so you'd have a sense of purpose."

"You did it to keep me busy," she answers.

"There's a difference?"

"You thought it would make me less angry."

"What happened, Lilliane?"

"We were infiltrated."

"*Infiltrated*? By what?"

"Humans," she answers. "Ordinary, desperate, fear-ridden, beautiful, mortal humans. Humans with fake identities and guns."

"I take it no one was hurt?"

"Well, you would have been able to sense it, right?" she asks. He has the ability to appear to any of them whenever he'd like, but beyond that, he's never disclosed how much of a real psychic connection exists between him and his bastard stepchildren. Can he sense their losses? Their rages? The glittering unfurling of the powers they unleash inside of The Desire Exchange?

He doesn't take the bait. But he doesn't vanish either. And he's had long enough to make his necessary mark on the suitcase.

"One of our radiants—his father sent people looking for him," she finally offers.

"I see," Bastian says quietly.

"Ryan Benoit. You remember Ryan Benoit, don't you?" This accusatory question hits its target; Bastian lowers his gaze. Did he also flinch? She can't be sure.

"Of course I remember, Ryan," he says quietly. "I remember all of you."

Radiants. He still has trouble with this word, given he didn't come up with it. So she decides to hit him with another word he's sure to find far more troubling.

"Your children, you mean," she says.

To this, Bastian betrays no response. He's never been able to refer to them as his offspring or anything of the sort; never been willing to claim them as family. No matter how kind he is to her, Lilliane is sure he regards her and the other radiants as nothing more than unfortunate accidents, the necessary downside of his incredible magic.

"Anyway," Lilliane says, satisfied to have struck two blows in a row, "it was a bit of a mess, but it's all worked out now."

"You're sure your secret's safe? Despite this incident?"

"We provided their ringleader with the same service we provide all of our clientele. She was quite happy with the result."

Lilliane cocks her head in the direction of the suitcase. Bastian pops it open.

Inside are six cushioned slots just large enough for the jars she brings him on a regular basis. Four of the slots are empty. But the golden radiance swirling within the two glass jars she did bring is strong enough to illuminate Bastian's face, an illumination that fills his hollow eyes, turning his pupils and sclera into vague gold outlines and not much else.

"Alexandra Vance," Lilliane says, tapping one jar. "Emily Blaine," she continues, tapping the one next to it.

"It doesn't matter," Bastian says quietly.

"*What* doesn't matter?"

"Their names. Who they came from. One batch is as good as the next. In the end, it's all the same energy. The bravery to face your heart's true desires. Once I add it to the candles, it finds who it needs to find."

"I see. And what about *my* candle, Bastian? The candle you sold me. Did it find who it needed to find?"

For a second, she thinks he's about to vanish just to avoid answering this question. But he's staring past her into the night sky, head cocked like a dog's at the sound of a whistle. She follows the direction of his gaze and sees three Mylar balloons rising into the night sky over Jackson Square; they're stamped with congratulatory expressions in bright letters: CONGRATULATIONS! AMAZING! GOOD WORK!

Bastian doesn't normally respond to an environmental intrusion in this quick and reflexive way. Something about these balloons means something to him. And when his entire being flickers, it seems to startle him as much as it does her. He looks down at his chest, checks the security of his grip on the suitcase's handle.

"Bastian," she asks quietly.

"It seems my services are soon to be required," he says meekly.

And then he's gone.

It's the first time she hasn't seen him disappear of his own accord.

Summoned, she finally thinks. *He was summoned. And he couldn't control it. He had no choice.* The sight of the man she holds responsible for her interminable fate rendered so suddenly powerless leaves her speechless. It almost makes her anger vanish as quickly as Bastian just did.

Almost.

6

LANEY

"So…." Michael says.

"So," Laney answers. Her phone buzzes in her pocket.

It's a text message from Cat.

Status update?

A horse drawn carriage clatters past them. In a high, barking voice, the driver recounts the history of the house and courtyard in which Perry's resides while Laney and Michael stand in front of the restaurant's entrance like awkward teenagers, the carriage passengers gawking at them like they're artifacts themselves. The Mylar balloons bob in the air just above Laney's head, the end of their strings tied around her right wrist. When the carriage finally moves on, they're left with boisterous knots of tourists filing past them in the direction of Bourbon Street, folks who don't have to worry about being awake for work or class in the morning, folks eager to burn the midnight oil in a city where the bars never close.

"Late for another date?" Michael asks.

Laney realizes she's been rudely staring at the phone in her hand.

"Yeah, I've got like seven tonight. Clients mostly."

"*Clients?*" Michael asks, barely able to contain his laughter.

"Yeah. I'm real popular with the rest of the faculty too."

"Oh!" he barks. "You went there. You totally went there."

"It's a friend of mine," Laney says. "She's checking up on me."

"Okay," Michael says. "Write her back. Tell her we got off to kind of a shaky start, and then after that, we played it safe for the rest of the meal and talked about stuff like our favorite TV shows from childhood and the weather. And now we're standing outside the restaurant and we're both thinking that while this would probably be the *safest* moment to call it a night, we've both had a little champagne, and we just had a ten minute discussion about whether or not an adult can use those baby wipes on himself on a regular basis without being called OCD. And so we're both afraid that if we end the date now, we're not going to make another one because every time we think of the other person we're going to see a toilet or a baby's butt or something."

"It sounds like you've had a lot more champagne than I have," she says.

"It *sounds* that way, but it's not technically true."

"This is true. Still, it's a little long for a text message."

"Well, what does she want to know?"

"Status update."

"Well, tell her it's going well. Tell her the story about Brooke isn't something I make up just to get into my student's pants."

"I thought we were past that."

"We are. Sort of. Anyway, don't tell her all that. Just tell her that we're both a little tipsy and we're going to take a walk through the Quarter to try to sober up. Which will be cool. 'Cause we'll be the first people in history who have ever tried to sober up in the French Quarter. *And—*"

"You have become a man of many words tonight, Michael Brouchard."

"*Become?* I lead a discussion section, Laney."

"True. What should I tell her for real?"

"Tell her we're going to be on crowded, well-lit streets the whole time if she'd like to follow us from twenty paces."

"Oh, I don't think she's going to follow us."

"She kind of already is. Isn't that her right there?"

Laney follows the direction of Michael's pointing finger and finds Cat waving at them from across the street as drunken tourists weave to avoid her. Her laptop and purse are slung over one shoulder.

"Cat Burke, right?" Michael says. "I taught her last year. We called her Cat Nap. One guess why."

"Hi, Mister Brouchard!" Cat calls from across the street.

"It's Michael, Cat. Just Michael. I'm a grad student. I don't teach high school."

"Uh-huh," Cat answers, then she sees Laney's glare and her smile fades. "CC's closed!"

"Okay," Laney answers.

"Uhm…I'm gonna go to Café du Monde. Maybe get some coffee."

"Sounds like a plan," Laney says. "You go have some coffee."

"Oh, I see!" Cat calls back. "Now you can't wait to get rid of me."

"Or you could just stop talking," Laney replies.

"*Bye!*"

They watch Cat hurry off down the crowded sidewalk. When Laney turns to face Michael, he gives her a crooked grin, his barely contained laughter causing the nostrils on his Roman nose to flare.

"I didn't ask her to do that," she says.

"Do what?"

"Wait around like that."

"She's protective of you. I'd say that's a point in her favor."

"Earlier she said she wouldn't come and get me if I didn't promise to have sex with you tonight."

"*Another* reason I'm a Cat Nap fan!"

"Let's walk, mister," she says, taking his hand in hers quickly, casually, before any of them can consider it a moment or a turning point. And suddenly they're walking hand-in-hand down the sidewalk toward Jackson Square as if they've done it their whole lives.

"I have an idea," Michael says.

"Shoot."

"I saw it on a TV show," he says.

"Which one?" she asks.

"Not saying."

"*What?*" she cries.

"No, seriously. You'll think I'm a giant nerd."

"Whatever. I didn't meet you tailgating. You're my teacher."

"Fine. It's from a *Doctor Who* Christmas special."

"Oh, wow. That is nerdy."

"It's a *great* show!" Michael whines.

"I've never seen it."

"Then don't judge. Please. I'm feeling really judged right now."

"I'm just teasing."

"I feel so vulnerable," he says in a meek, small voice. "Is this how women feel all the time?"

"Keep it up with the sexist jokes and the last you'll feel of me will be my hand coming out of yours."

"I'm not a nerd," he whines.

"Yes, you are. And it's kind of what makes you sexy."

"Good. 'Cause where I come from, nerds weren't considered sexy."

"Well, where I come from, there weren't any nerds. Just crystal meth dealers. And in my book, sexy men have teeth and they don't think the wires in their house are talking to them."

"Yikes."

"Yeah. So what was this…uhm, *Doctor Who*-related idea you wanted to run by me? Time travel?"

"You *have* seen the show!" Michael cries.

"Maybe one episode. I don't know. I mean, I haven't seen all the Christmas specials like you have. Nerd."

"Never mind," he mutters. "It's a stupid idea."

"Oh, my God. Don't do a baby voice. Now I feel terrible."

"Okay. It goes like this. We ask each other a series of questions. But the person answering can only answer with one word."

"What about the person asking the questions?" Laney asks.

"The question can be as long as you want. But the answer can only be—"

"One word!" Laney finishes for him.

"That's right."

"Got it. Who goes first?"

A gang of drunken frat boys are heading straight for them, and for a second, she fears they're going to have to separate to let them pass. But when she starts to pull her hand free from Michael's, he tightens his grip and at the last minute, the frat boys realize they're up against an iron wall. They part on either side of the determined couple while Laney savors Michael's resolute grip, the raw evidence of his determination not to let her go over something trivial and inconvenient.

"You first," Michael says. "We'll do five-and-five."

"I get to ask five questions, then you ask five?"

"Yep."

"Okay—"

"Also, no follow-up questions," he adds.

"Wait. What do you mean?"

"I mean an answer can only be one word. If you want clarification, you have to ask another completely different question."

"All right. Let's start before you make any more rules," Laney says.

"And no yes-or-no questions."

"Oh my God!"

"It'll make sense once we start playing. Trust me."

"*If* we start playing."

"I'm done making up rules. I promise. Hit me."

"Okay," she says. "What will you be doing with your life in five years?"

There's a few seconds of silence between them, punctuated by sounds of their footfalls and the balloons rubbing together in the air behind her.

"Loving," he says.

Her heart races and her breath catches and the restraints of the game become instantly clear and make her dizzy. *Loving who? Loving what? Loving how? Loving…her?* But follow-up questions aren't allowed. Leading yes-or-no questions are also out.

"Where do you see yourself living?" she asks.

He starts to answer, then stops himself, probably because he was about to break one of his own rules.

"Italy," he says. He grunts in his throat and purses his lips. She wonders if the answer's more specific than he liked, but rules are rules, after all.

"What's the one thing you can't do without?" she asks him.

"Food," he answers.

"What's the one thing you can't do without aside from food, water, and shelter?"

"Follow-up question," he says with a low growl.

"I'm allowed one each round."

"That's a new rule."

"That's right," she answers. "It's my rule."

He grunts.

"Love," he says.

One question left. This round, anyway.

"What was the first thing you thought when you saw me?" she asks.

"Finally," he answers.

His simple, elegant answer knocks the wind out of her. Can he feel her come close to losing her footing? They're paces away from Jackson Square, and he hasn't missed a step.

"My turn," he says. They're passing through the deep shadows under a townhouse's second floor balcony, but she can hear the hint of a smile in his restrained tone.

"Ready," she says, even though she feels anything but.

But by the time they've entered Jackson Square, he still hasn't asked her a question, which leaves her wondering if he's done with this game. If his final, dizzying answer was all the pretext he needs to take her face in his hands and—

"What's your biggest fear?"

"Failure," she answers without a second thought.

And as the word just hangs there, suddenly the limitations of the game infuriate her. She's aching to give a more specific answer. To tell him what *kind* of failure she means. But refusing to give into this urge forces her to question it, and suddenly all her qualifications, her desire to specify and narrow it down to *one kind* of failure seem full of duplicity. She's always wanted to do everything perfectly; that's the long and short of it. When people tell her there's no perfect way to do anything, she usually blocks out their words with a plastic smile and a series of nods.

They're walking along one side of the cast-iron fence girding the center of the square and hung with cityscape paintings and caricature sketches by the street artists who have set up shop along the flagstones. She can already smell the horses lined up along Decatur Street. But Michael's grip feels lackluster all of a sudden. When she glances down at their hands, she sees he's holding her hand just as tightly as he was before. It's her own thoughts and fears that have made him feel suddenly faraway. Maybe that's another point of the game—to give the most honest and authentic answer, and then force yourself to remain present in your own skin.

"What do you want most in the world?" he asks.

"Security," she says.

She sucks in a deep breath, tightens her grip on his hand.

"Is this hard for you?" he asks.

"No yes-or-no questions."

"Sorry. Give me a sec."

A second passes. Then another second passes. Then another…

"If you could live anywhere in the world, where would you live?" he asks.

"Italy," she answers.

His hand jerks in hers. He makes a low throaty grunt that sounds satisfied.

When they reach Dumaine Street, he pulls her to their right and suddenly they're walking past a long row of horse-drawn carriages sitting idly at the foot of the square. They're also walking away from the bright lights and green awnings of Café du Monde across the street, where Cat currently waits for her somewhere amidst the crowd of camera-toting tourists with shirtfronts dusted by the powdered sugar that's slipped off their beignets with every bite.

Two more questions in this round.

He's sure taking his sweet time coming up with them.

"What's the one thing you can't live without?" he asks.

There's no rule against asking a question that's been asked of you, so she decides to answer.

"Truth," she says.

Not love, she realizes. *He said love and you didn't say love. And maybe that's okay. Maybe you don't have to have exactly the same answers for him to...* She doesn't want to finish that sentence. But she does anyway. In her head. About a dozen different times. *For him to want you, kiss you, need you,* love *you.*

"Describe your family in one word," he says.

"Distant," she answers.

They're heading back in the direction of St. Louis Cathedral, and for some reason this side of the square is quieter. Maybe because the shadows offered by the oak branches overhead are longer and darker.

"Your turn," he says quietly.

"If you could be anything in the world right now besides a teacher, what would it be?"

"Artist," he answers.

"If you could be any animal in the world, which one would you be?"

"Eagle," he answers.

"Really?"

"No follow-ups. You've got three more."

Her heart races. Her face feels hot.

"If you could do one thing to me right now, what would it be?" she asks.

The cold metal of one of the fence posts presses up against her back, and that's when she realizes he's taken her into his embrace. His hands, his powerful, kneading hands, grip her waist, making the loose fabric of her dress feel as insubstantial as a blush of humidity. He brings their mouths and bodies together with the hunger of a hundred class sessions, a hundred long looks, a hundred fevered daydreams. As soon as she tastes him for the first time, she realizes the real question isn't whether or not the passion between them is wrong or right, but how long would they be able to resist it?

She grips the back of his head, slides her fingers to the back of his thick, powerful neck. There's that smell, his smell. Maybe it's his cologne, or maybe it's some intermingling of scents that are more purely, naturally *him*. Vanilla, campfires, and something musky. Only when she feels his palm grip the underside of her thigh does she realize she's about to wrap her right leg around his waist, that her dress is sliding up her leg and if she doesn't lower it soon she'll be exposing herself right in the middle of Jackson Square.

Their lips part. He cups her face in his hands. She slides her leg back to the ground, slowly so as not to send the false message that his touch is repulsive; she just can't risk exposing herself to passersby.

"You have two more questions," he growls.

"Will you wait?" she asks.

"For?"

"One word answers only. Remember?"

"Yeah, and no yes-or-no questions either, remember? You still want to play this game?"

"It was your game, professor."

"And you were being a very good bad little student."

"Will you wait, Michael?"

"I already said I would."

"Michael…" Her hands find his face, and somehow this touch feels more forbidden and electrifying than their passionate kiss, just allowing her fingers to gently rest against the hard angles of his face she's studied day after day in class. To feel the heat of him in this gentle and unhurried way.

"Laney," he says, in a gentle imitation of her own breathless voice.

"Even if I make you wait forever?"

"Is that your plan?" he asks quietly. But he's taken his hands away from her flaming cheeks, and suddenly it seems awkward to continue touching his face when he's just released her own, and just like that, with just one slightly disjointed question, there's a foot of distance between that feels like a mile. "To make me wait forever?" he asks.

A minute goes by before she realizes she hasn't answered, hasn't said anything to assuage his fears. She's been so damn focused on her own. The slight distance between them is enough to allow every muscle in her body to knot with tension, a tension so uniform and persistent there's no mistaking it for what it truly is—resistance.

When he takes her hands in his again, he's not preparing for another passionate embrace. It feels like he's comforting her.

"So I guess this is where this night ends?" he asks.

"I need—I mean, I just need…"

Deep breath. Deep breath. If she could just get one more deep breath. The sensations throughout her body feel like a terrible moment of self-realization; passion and panic sit side-by-side within her fundamental being, and she's going to have to learn how to separate them.

"Cat's waiting for you at Café du Monde, right? You want me to walk you over there?"

"No. I'm fine."

She is so obviously and clearly *not* fine that this response renders Michael silent.

A panic attack. Is that what's happening? Is she literally having a panic attack because the most beautiful, amazing man she's ever met has just promised to take her fears away? She's become that woman she used to sneer at in movies, the one who can't accept a gift from the universe, the one so full of fear and anxiety she can't take a chance on anything. How can that be? That's not Laney Foley. Laney clawed her way out of a neighborhood of people who thought she was personally insulting them by reading books. She worked three jobs at once to put herself through community college, applied for every scholarship she could. Aren't *those* the parts of life that are supposed to terrify people, paralyze people? Not the possibility of being loved by an amazing man.

But for her, passion could be dangerous, couldn't it? This kind of a passion in particular.

A teacher's passion.

She hasn't read the fine print of her scholarship agreement, because she doesn't want to read the goddamn fine print on her scholarship agreement, thank you very much. She's been so damn focused on the idea of Michael punishing her with a bad grade if things didn't work out, she hasn't stopped to consider whether her own scholarship involves a real consequence for going to bed with someone responsible for her grade. Even if it were only an allegation, brought by him, or anyone, or a jerk like Jake Briffel, what would happen if she were accused of trading sex for grades to maintain her status in the university's most exclusive and competitive scholarship?

Now there are black spots crowding her vision, darker and more menacing than the shadows all around him. It feels like she's breathing through a straw. And her arms, shoulders and neck are tingling. Not sensual, anticipatory tingles. This is oxygen deprivation as a result of hyperventilation. This is anxiety and fear run amuck in her veins.

Yep. Definitely a panic attack.

"I'll be fine," she says, pulling away from the fence and from him.

"Laney?"

"Just. Please. I need a …"

Her feet finish the sentence for her.

She's already broken into a run when she realizes that's exactly what she's doing. Running. She is literally running away from the man of her dreams, away from the sound of his voice calling out to her, his struggle over whether or not to chase her evident in his pained sounding cry. Only once she's left Jackson Square in her dust does she realize what the slight tug on her right wrist meant as she took off. She snagged the balloon's strings on the fence as she ran, releasing them into the night sky.

7

He's right behind me, Laney thinks. But when she turns, she finds herself on a shadowy, side street with blurry, disjointed memories of how she got here. And Michael is nowhere to be seen.

She remembers racing across Bourbon Street, darting through thick crowds, dodging a mounted policeman whose horse expelled hot breath on one side of her face in a terrible burst. She ran with the conviction that each pounding step would drive the breath back into her lungs, flush the ice-cold prickles from her skin. To some degree it's worked. She's gasping now instead of wheezing. But she's also alone and too close to Rampart Street, the Quarter's northern boundary.

Silly of her to think Michael would have been able to keep up, not without drawing the attention of cops on Bourbon. That's how fast she was running, and if he'd run that fast to keep up, what would we have looked like? Even in flats, her near-sprint has left her feet throbbing with pain.

Still, why did she stop right *here*? Why was she suddenly overcome by the sense that he was just a few feet away??

I can smell him, she realizes. *I can smell him as strongly as if I were still in his arms. Vanilla and campfires and some kind of spice I can't name.*

Several second-floor balconies cover the depth of the sidewalk, their filigree ironwork dappling the street with scatters of shadows. A strange glow emanates from the windows of the tiny shop across the street. The glow is just faint enough for her to make out the wood-plank sign hanging over the open door and the gold outline of a tiny candle flame. The shelves inside the front window are lined with uniform candles, each one so large she could hold one in both hands, one hand on each side of the glass, and her fingers wouldn't touch.

A candle shop open at this hour, this far from the main drag?

But it's the source of the smell, Michael's smell. It has to be. Just to be sure, she pulls a piece of her dress close to her nose. Maybe his cologne rubbed off on her during their embrace and she's coated with the stuff. But her dress smells more like dinner than the man of her dreams. When she lifts her head again, when she gazes across the street at the quaint little candle shop bathed in a gold light that feels otherworldly, a tide of it hits her again.

With each step she takes toward the shop, she feels as if she's slipped further out of her own body.

It's only the second day of class and he's asked them to meet him at the sculpture garden at the New Orleans Museum of Art in City Park. He's telling them how art is something that's present in their everyday lives, not just something you visit in museums or study in books. The bright sculptures shining in the sunlight all around them are proof of that. And that's when she realizes he's not like any other man she's ever known, as she gazes up at him, sitting cross-legged on the grass with the other students as he speaks. Handsome and brilliant and full of passion for something besides football. That was when she first caught his particular smell and it felt like he had unzipped her soul without touching her. And the moment had been so intoxicating, so powerful, she'd shoved it down and repressed it, and now it's coming back to her unfiltered, uncensored, overpowering and raw.

She knocks on the doorway's frame. There's no answer.

The shop before her is tiny, but too beautiful and immaculate to have been carelessly abandoned at this late hour. Instead of a register or counter, there's a small desk tucked in one corner beneath a row of ribbon wheels attached to the wall above. A large black table with a round marble top takes up the center of the tiny space. The table's curvilinear supports make her think of snakes, if you made snakes rounded and elegant and lined their bodies with tiny flecks of ivory.

The source of the smell is sitting on a metal tray, a few inches from a vase exploding with yellow flowers she doesn't recognize. It's a candle just like the ones lining the shelves in the front window, only this one is lit. And the smell coming from it is *Michael.*

"Good evening," a male voice says.

She cries out, startled. The man suddenly standing a few feet away only smiles. She can't decide if he's handsome or just pretty. His outfit looks so formal and out-of-date she wonders if he's some kind of tour guide. Most of the tour groups she's spotted that evening were led by women dressed like vampires, but maybe there's a Jazz Age walking tour of the Quarter she's never heard of. Because with his purple silk vest, his linen tailored slacks, and his slicked-back, side-parted hair, the Jazz Age is exactly where this man seems to belong.

"What is this?" she asks, pointing to the candle. She hasn't just asked. She's barked it. At the sound of her tense, frightened anger, the shopkeeper doesn't flinch or recoil. Instead, he gives her a placating smile, as if her harsh question were an enticement to learn more about her.

"It's a candle," he says.

"I know it's a candle. But what's the smell. I mean, what's it made of?"

"Would you like to sit down, miss?"

"No. I don't want to sit down. I want you to tell me what's in this candle. *Please*."

She can hear the strain in her voice, the losing battle against tears.

"The human brain is a mysterious thing," the man says. "Smells trigger memory, mostly, and so I would suggest that the individual ingredients are irrelevant. Irrelevant to the experience you're having right now."

"Irrelevant?"

"Forgive me, I don't mean to dismiss your feelings. I suggest that their source might be somewhat larger than what's contained in that candle."

"Yeah, but…"

This is insane. Is she really about to explain Michael's aroma to this strange man?

"I was with a man earlier and he…"

"He was what?"

"He smelled like this candle. Just like it. Look, I'm sorry. I don't mean to sound so crazy."

"In the Quarter, at this hour, you'd have to work rather hard to seem like the crazy ones."

She laughs in spite of herself.

"Right. But still…I just, I really need you to tell me what's in it. Can you just tell me…?" *Because I'm suddenly afraid that this smell is all I'll ever be able to have of him, the only piece of Michael I might be able to keep.*

"This man," the candlemaker asks. "Did he upset you?"

"Did he *upset* me?" The strain in her voice turns into a stammer. She tries to wipe tears but it feels like she's missing each one. "No. No, he didn't upset me. He did everything perfectly. He did everything right. But he's…"

"He's what?"

"It's not possible," she says. "He's my teacher."

"Oh, I see. So he's considerably older than you?"

"Three years. Not that old."

"And he'll be your teacher for the rest of your natural life, of course."

"He's not big on waiting."

"So he's refused to wait?"

"No. He hasn't *refused* to wait. It's just that—"

"What? What has he done that's upset you so?"

"Nothing. He hasn't done anything to upset me, other than be exactly what I want."

"The miserable bastard," the candlemaker whispers with a smile.

His smile is disarming and Laney finds herself laughing through her tears.

"Can you please just tell me what's in this candle so I'll stop losing my mind?"

"You think that'll do it, do you?"

"Easy, fella. We just met."

"I see. Well, it's a proprietary blend, designed to stimulate certain areas of the brain which ignite passion."

"Are you serious? Is that what's on your marketing materials?"

The candlemaker gestures to a notecard taped to one side the candle's glass container. "No. It's much simpler actually," she says.

Laney lifts the notecard's flap and reads the calligraphy within.

Light this flame at the scene of your greatest passion and your heart's desire will be yours.

"I'm Bastian," the man says. "Bastian Drake."

He extends his hand. She takes it gently in her own, sees the skin on his fingers is remarkably smooth. The guy looks like he must be in his twenties, but he talks like he's from a bygone era.

"Laney," she answers. "Laney Foley."

"Take it," he says.

"Excuse me?"

"The candle. Take it. It's yours."

"I can't afford it."

"You can because it's a gift."

"Seriously?"

"I am."

"You'll get in trouble."

"With who? I own this place."

"Seriously."

"My stars, you aren't very good at accepting gifts, are you?"

"In my experience they come with *rules*."

"Rules? Like don't fall in love with your teacher? A rule that I'm sure has *never* been broken before."

"I'm on a scholarship. A good one. If I do anything to screw it up—"

"Then what?"

"Then I'm back on the West Bank busting my ass to find a job while my family tells me over and over again how I was an idiot to try for something better. How I don't really love them because I want a different life for myself."

"I see. But if you follow the *rules*, everything will be perfect, right?"

"If I keep my scholarship, I've got a shot."

"And even if you waited until this man was no longer your teacher, you still think it would endanger your scholarship."

"People might talk."

"I see. So it's not just your scholarship. You're also afraid of what people will think."

"You know what I mean."

"I do. I do know what you mean. Fear doesn't come from our circumstances. It comes from within. And that means we can change our circumstances and fix what we think is the problem, and the fear will still be there, waiting to be dealt with."

"And how do you deal with it?"

"You stop living in a dozen different imaginary futures and you start living in today."

"Oh, everyone says that like it's so easy."

"No, actually. Everyone says it because it's something we all need to do a better job of, and we need to do a better job of it because it's incredibly difficult."

Thanks, Yoda. But she's glad she doesn't say it because it would be intolerably rude given how nice this man is being. But she wouldn't be Laney Foley if she didn't have some sort of comeback.

"I got where I am today by focusing on the *future*," she says.

"Indeed, and wherever it is you are today, Miss Foley, it seems like a very painful place."

His response has silenced her and this seems to please him. He picks up the lit candle in both hands. She waits for him to blow it out, but instead he pinches the flame itself between two impossibly smooth fingers, then he moves to his tiny desk. When he begins packaging it for her in a brightly colored paper bag complete with tissue paper and an elaborate clover of turquoise and purple ribbon, her mouth opens to protest. Even though his back is turned, he must have heard her sharp intake of breath because he says, "Not another word."

"You're a strange man, Mister Drake."

"Of this," he says, turning, a disarming smile on his youthful face, "I am most certainly aware, Miss Foley."

When she takes the bag from his hand, she glimpses some sort of pulse of gold light in both of his eyes, probably a trick thrown by a pair of passing headlights outside. But for there to be passing headlights, you would need to have a passing car, and the street outside is utterly silent. Something has just happened right behind her, however, because just then Bastian's smile fades and his gaze cuts to the shop's entrance.

The beautiful, full-figured woman standing in the doorway wears a black leather dress several shades lighter than her own skin. Her fixed, stony expression is impossible for Laney to read. Her first guess is that she's a jealous wife or girlfriend who has mistaken their exchange for flirtation. But this has less to do with the woman's rigid posture and intent gaze and more to do with Bastian's apparent shock at seeing her on his doorstep.

"Good evening," the woman says.

Then Laney remembers she's a tear-splotched, disheveled mess who just ran clear across the French Quarter in the throes of a panic attack. Maybe that's why the woman's studying her with something that looks vaguely like disdain.

"Hi," Laney says quietly. Then to Bastian, whose gaze is still fixated on their visitor, she says, "Thank you, Mister Drake."

"Bastian," he answers, his reflexive politeness still in effect even as he refuses to take his eyes off the beautiful black woman a few feet away.

"Thank you, Bastian."

At the last possible second, the woman steps aside and allows Laney to leave the shop. But a few paces from the entrance, Laney feels eyes on the back of her neck. She turns, sees the woman is staring after her with that same haunting, unreadable expression on her face.

8

LILLIANE

"What's her name?" Lilliane asks, as she watches the young woman hurry off into the night.

"Lilliane, don't—"

"What's her name, Bastian?"

When she started searching, Lilliane assumed there was very little chance she'd actually find the shop. It rarely materializes in the same place twice and she's fairly sure it vanishes as soon as Bastian delivers his special gift to his latest victim. So the shock of seeing it all again—the round black marble-topped table, the vase of strange yellow flowers, the ribbon wheels above the tiny, makeshift desk, all of it looking exactly as it did on that long-ago afternoon— has left her stunned.

Nothing, however, could have prepared her for the act of witnessing an exchange just like the one that changed the very fabric of her being decades before. It was one thing to know they'd been happening every so often over the past fifty-six years, but seeing one unfold right before her eyes has filled her with a strange blend of sadness and anger for which she has no name. Part of her is terrified the woman will meet a fate similar to her own, the other is filled with bitter jealousy over the prospect that she will not.

"Laney," Bastian says. "Laney Foley."

"Do you know their names before you appear to them? Is that how it works?"

He doesn't answer. He just stands there in the middle of his rapidly assembled stage-set of a shop like a perfectly put-together street performer. "Did you know my name, Bastian?"

"No."

"I see. Well, I'm going to keep an eye on her." Lilliane descends several steps until she can spot the girl's shrinking silhouette blending with the bright smear of lights of Bourbon Street. "I'll make sure she makes the right decision."

"It's possible your intervention will be of no use."

"Well, if you've taught me anything, Bastian, it's that anything's possible."

"Lilliane, don't let your anger guide you."

"Don't speak to me of my anger!"

She whirls to face him, finds herself staring at the grimy front door to an abandoned store. Just a few inches from her nose, a dusty FOR LEASE signs tilts to one side against the filthy glass.

Bastian is gone. The candles are gone. It's no use arguing with a being who can stop time.

Fair enough. She's got work to do.

9

LANEY

Laney isn't surprised to wake up in her dorm room alone. Her roommate, Perfect Skinny Kelley, as Cat calls her, is carrying on two love affairs at the same time: one with her boyfriend, the other with her boyfriend's off-campus apartment.

Thanks to both of her roommate's lovers, Laney didn't have to endure any complaints about the overpowering scent of Bastian Drake's candle when she got home the night before, and this morning there's no one around to tease her for printing out Michael's late night e-mail and reading it over and over and again until her eyelids grew heavy and she fell asleep on the paper like a child cuddling a stuffed animal.

Berry Hall is one of the older dorms on campus, a blocky ten-story high-rise with crappy AC made bearable by huge, easily opened windows that allow her to fill the room with a nice cool breeze. Did she leave one of them open last night? Her alarm clock isn't set to go off for another forty minutes, but she is jerked awake with such force it's like the damn thing is already squealing right next to her head. Maybe a sound from outside is to blame. But when she reaches behind the Pottery Barn curtains and feels for the window handles, she finds them both shut tight.

The first item on her morning agenda is three cups of coffee from the Kelley's Keurig—Kelley has charitably allowed her four a day—and a good hour-and-a-half of work on her Geology paper before hauling it across campus to her lecture for History of the Americas II. That was the plan she made at the beginning of the week anyway, before she had a date with her teacher, before she suffered her first full-on panic attack.

Maybe it was the intensity of her dreams that awakened her, dreams of Michael's lips, fingers, eyes, and tongue, or maybe she'd finally had enough of the puddle of drool in between her cheek and the paper on which she printed out Michael's e-mail.

Or maybe it's frickin' Maybelline for all she cares.

The only thing she feels like doing now is reading his e-mail for the seven-hundredth time.

So I realized after I lost track of you that I don't actually have your phone number, which meant I couldn't call. There's a fine line between chasing and stalking and I don't want to cross it, which means I wasn't going to track you down at your dorm. I know that's what the guy in a movie would have done. But honestly, that's a reason to call campus security, right? (Also, I think I had too much to eat because it was clear after I chased you for half a block I was never going to be able to catch up with you without barfing. I thought the only thing worse than catching up with you if you didn't want to be caught would be catching up with you covered in barf. Agree?) I will say, aside from being an excellent student, you're an incredible runner, Miss Foley. So here's my phone number. (It's right here. See? 555-7639.) If you're done with me, you can throw it away and everything will go back to normal. Promise. If heartbroken is your idea of normal. : (Don't worry. I'm a big boy, I'll get over it. But if this is my last chance to say this, here goes. You are an amazing woman who isn't giving herself enough credit for how remarkable she is. It would be amazing if you gave me the opportunity to tell you that every day (or every other day, or maybe every other three days until we hit the six month mark. Whatever Cat decides is "healthy.") But if you're not able to give me the chance, please print out that sentence and keep it on a card in your wallet and read it when things are getting you down. In fact, I'll type it over with a space and a fun font so it looks better when you

take it out and read it on a crappy day. Like this:

You are an amazing woman who isn't giving herself enough credit for how remarkable she is. — M. B.

Yours In Comic Sans,
Michael

P.S. I was tempted to put my phone number right next to the quote above so you'd never forget it. I think professional artists call that branding.

If only he could have been a jerk about the whole thing.

If only he could have been defensive and angry and hurt, all things some childish part of her probably wanted from him as soon as she took off the night before.

But, no. Even in the face of her crazy, he's humble and self-effacing and attuned to appropriate boundaries and intelligent and charming as ever.

Her laptop—Cat's old laptop computer that Cat gave to her at the beginning of the year when she upgraded her own—chimes at the arrival of a new e-mail.

When she sees the message isn't from Michael, her heart drops a little. Then she sees it's from the office manager for the undergraduate art history program and her heart drops more than a little.

Please call the office immediately regarding your discussion section for Foundations of Western Art II.

As she listens to the phone ring, her breaths are short and shallow. And by the time the woman on the other end answers, Laney is stammering a greeting and clearing her throat at the same time.

"This is Laney Foley," she finally manages. "I have, uhm, an e-mail from you guys about my discussion section."

"Right, right, right," the woman says quickly while tapping keys on her computer. Whoever she is, her caffeine levels are at peak, while Laney is still struggling to open both eyes. "Let me get this up here on my screen. Give me a second."

"Sure," Laney says.

He lost it. I didn't write him back last night and he lost it and now he's going to punish me. The e-mail was bullshit and now the axe is going to—-

"Yeah, here we go," the woman says. "He says you two talked about some sort of scheduling problem that's started to come up for you on Wednesdays. Does that sound familiar?"

"Uh-huh," she grunts.

No. Oh, my God. What's happening?

"And so he thought it would be best if the department moved you to a different discussion section. So I went ahead and checked your schedule and it looks like you've got an opening on Friday, and it just so happens we've got another discussion section we could move you into then. But it's with a different T.A. Kimberly Stockton."

"Is that allowed? Moving me into a class with a different teacher?"

"Yes. It's just a discussion section. They follow the same syllabus."

"Sure. Right. Yeah."

What the hell are you doing, Michael?

"Your final grade will be an average of the grades Michael gave you in his Wednesday class, and what you receive from Kimberly in the Friday class."

"So Michael won't give me my final grade. Kimberly will."

"Kimberly will be grading your final three assignments and at the end of the semester, those will be averaged with the grades you've already received from Michael. Does that make sense?"

"Yeah. Yeah it does."

What he said to her the night before? He couldn't take away her fears if she didn't give him the chance. Well, that was bunk. He'd just removed one of her biggest fears with a single e-mail to his department.

Then why am I still so goddamn afraid?

Laney pretends to listen as the woman explains how it will take a few days for the system to reflect the schedule change, but that next Friday she should report to Kimberly's class and here's the name of the classroom where Kimberly Stockton's discussion section meets and—blah blah blah.

Instead, she hears her pulse pounding in her ears, bringing with it the terrible realization that it's just like Bastian Drake said to her the night before. The fear is still there. The fear comes from within her, not from Michael, not from the art history department, not from the Rose Scholarship.

I'm not good enough.

There it is. A voice clear as a bell, a voice that sounds like her mother, her father, and all of her cousins rolled into one, a voice that speaks to her so clearly and with words that sound so carefully chosen, how could she *not* listen to it? How could she not heed its angry, hurtful advice?

You can go to as nice a school as you want, little girl, but it won't change the fact that you are poor white trash putting on airs and he's gonna smell this on you every day while you smell vanilla and campfires, and then he's gonna drop you like a cold, hard stone.

Is she still on the campus health plan? What are the names of the antidepressants she's heard other students talk about, the ones that actually work? Phrases like "anxiety disorder" and "panic syndrome" are dancing together in her brain now, as she tries to come up with any possible solution to this relentless, mental assault. If she didn't have a class in a few hours and a paper due next week, she'd probably head for the nearest bar. But instead she claws her hands through her hair and tilts her head forward and draws a deep breath through her nose.

And without meaning to, she inhales the scent of the candle at the foot of her bed.

The sunlight bounces off the chrome sculpture nearby, fills his eyes briefly before he blinks and smiles and continues with his passionate lecture. And she's so hypnotized by his beauty, she's stopped nervously picking at the grass next to her. And when he sees her looking up at him, he locks eyes with her and smiles, smiles longer than any teacher should at a student.

"What the fuck *are* you candle?" she hears herself saying.

Laney unties the bow so she can part the bag's handles, then she removes enough of the tissue paper to pull the candle free. She sets it on her bed and stares at it as if it's a kitten about to take its first steps. Wide veins of purple and brown are threaded through the wax. Twelve hours later and the scent has the same effect of delivering her straight to the sculpture garden outside the New Orleans Museum of Art, to the moment when her heart first opened to Michael.

She figured the notecard taped to the side was just for display and expected Bastian to remove it before packaging up the candle. But he left it right where it was when she wandered into his shop.

Light this flame at the scene of your greatest passion and your heart's desire will be yours.

She doesn't believe in magic or spells or voodoo. She *does* believe in following advice, and a lot of the advice Bastian gave her last night sounded good. No, *wise*. Experienced. So why not follow the flowery, romantic instruction printed on this card?

Sure, it sounds like the making of some silly little spell, something her crazy aunts might do for a sick relative or a friend who'd been cheated on. But sometimes stuff like that could have a placebo effect. And right now, she would try anything to silence these viciously critical voices running riot in her head.

Anything.

It takes all that self-control she's got, but she waits until after her lecture to text him. She's moved into the shady overhang of one of the older buildings fringing the Quad, far from the other students lounging on the grass during an unseasonably warm afternoon.

Looks like you're not my teacher anymore.

Just seven words, but they took fifteen minutes to write.

Cat's got one of those thought bubble logos that tells you if the other person has started typing in response to your text. Laney's old school cell phone has no such feature, and people often marvel at how fast she can fire off text messages using a regular telephone keypad.

So Laney waits. And waits. And waits. And then feels stupid for waiting because she sure as hell took her sweet time texting him back and maybe he's teaching or—

I hope you're not upset.

Three minutes. Not a bad response time for a guy who was walked out on—make that *run* out on—the night before. And then another one follows right on its digital heels.

Kimberly's a good egg. Just don't say anything negative about cubism. She's kind of obsessed.

Noted, Laney responds.

So the next time we go out to dinner it won't be as teacher and student. It'll just be a date with a guy who's crazy about you.

The breath leaves her. She rests her head against the stone column next to her.

If there's going to be a next time…

Then, just as she lifts her fingers to type, he responds again.

Maybe there's another barrier you need me to remove. Just say the word.

Before she can think twice, she starts tapping keys.

I'm not the biggest fan of my history teacher. Can you rub him

out for me?

Too jokey, too soon?

Sorry. Assassinations are a third date thing.

Laney explodes with tension-releasing laughter, so high and barking it draws the attention of a guitar player strumming for adoring freshman a few yards away.

Why are you so perfect? she types.

I'm not, he responds. ***I just try to be when I meet someone worth trying for.***

She's about to respond when she feels a strange prickling on the side of her face. Her index finger hovers over the keypad. She looks up, tries to find the source of this strange feeling.

The guitar player's gone back to performing for his adoring fans. But further away, across the Quad…

It can't be.

It's the woman from last night, the one Bastian Drake was startled to find standing in the entrance to his tiny shop. The one who wouldn't smile or introduce herself, who studied Laney with a cold, unreadable look. She's too far away for Laney to read her facial expression now, but she stands just as proudly. Her outfit is more casual, a cream-colored sleeveless peasant dress that billows around her generous frame. Some sort of jeweled headband sits on her dark hair like a glittering tiara.

Right now, she is more afraid of leaving Michael in the lurch then some jealous stalker girlfriend.

I would very much like to have dinner again.

An instant response. He must have been waiting on pins and needle for her text.

Is tonight too soon?

There goes her breath, and here comes her pulse.

She remembers the panic that threatened her just that morning, an attack that promised to be as powerful as the one she'd suffered the night before in Michael's arms. Then she remembers what ended it.

Light this flame at the scene of your greatest passion and your heart's desire will be yours.

It's not too soon, she types.

But first I need to do a magic spell a strange man in the French Quarter gave me because I think it might prevent me from having another panic attack when you kiss me.

K. Teaching right now so I'll get back to you about a plan ;)

The knowledge that he took time out from an actual class to send her all those texts makes her giddy. And this reminds her that he's no longer her teacher, no longer responsible for her grade, which makes her even giddier. Then she remembers her audience across the Quad. But when she looks up, the woman is gone. Maybe she imagined her. Given her mental state over the past twelve hours, she wouldn't be all that surprised.

All right, Mister Drake. Let's see if your candle's all it's cracked up to be.

She actually considered carrying the candle around in her backpack for the rest of the day. That way she could head straight to the sculpture garden after class and be done with this nonsense. But the overpowering scent would have earned her far too many angry looks as it washed over the library and then the lecture hall, that's for sure. So she's got no choice but to head back to her dorm room, praying under her breath that Kelley didn't come home earlier than expected and throw the thing out because she hated the smell. God knows, Cat bitched to high heaven when Laney had stepped into her car with it the night before. And it hadn't been the scent of vanilla and campfires that had earned Cat's ire either.

"Why would anyone make a candle that smells like a dirty fish tank?" Cat asked.

A special recipe intended to stimulate the centers of the brain that promote passion.

Isn't that what Bastian Drake had told her? That or something similarly dramatic. But if the candle smelled so different to Cat's nose than to Laney's, maybe that gave some truth to Bastian's self-promoting ridiculousness.

"Laney Foley."

She didn't imagine it. The beautiful black woman from the night before is standing a few feet away, just steps from the entrance to Laney's dorm.

"I need to speak with you," the woman says. "It's important."

"Listen, I don't know what you think was happening last night. But he just gave me a candle. That's all. I've never seen him before and I'll probably never see him again. He seemed nice, but apparently he's not all that nice if you think he's—anyway. Just a candle. That's all. I promise."

"It is *not* just a candle," the woman answers.

"Ma'am, please. I've had kind of a rough day and I just...I don't mean to be rude, I just *really* don't need any more drama right now."

"If you don't want any *drama* in your life, then *don't* light that candle."

If the woman really thinks Laney slept with her man, where's her self-righteous outrage? She seems conflicted. Like there's more she wants to say, but can't.

"What is it?" Laney asks. "A bomb?"

"No."

"Poison? *Drugs*?

"Is there somewhere we can talk?"

"I'll throw it away. How does that sound? As soon as I get upstairs, I'll throw it in the trash. And we're done, and it's all good."

"No. We're not *all good*."

"Okay. I've said my piece and I'm done, so I'm gonna go. Take care and please don't follow me or else I'll call campus security. Have a nice afternoon."

And with that, she starts for the entrance to her dorm. In what feels like one motion, Laney slides her keycard through the reader, steps inside the foyer and pulls the glass door shut behind her with both hands. When she turns, the woman's nowhere to be seen. Just a loose smattering of students on the distant lawn. She should still call someone, campus security maybe? File some kind of stalking report. If that's even a thing.

The elevator's on the tenth floor and she doesn't feel like waiting for it so she bounds up the fire staircase to her room on the seventh. The door is open a crack which must mean Kelley's home. Laney pulls the knob, already scripting a speech for Kelley about how they should all be on the lookout for a strange woman who just stopped her outside and probably thinks she banged her weird, Jazz Age-obsessed boyfriend.

As soon as Laney steps into her dorm room, the woman in question turns from the open window as if she's been waiting patiently for several minutes. A scream reaches the bottom of Laney's throat. The woman raises one index finger and quietly says, "Please don't scream, Laney. Everything will be all right if you just listen to me."

10

"*What the fuck?*"

"Is the language necessary?" her visitor asks.

"Yes. What the *fuck?*"

"I guess it's preferable to screaming."

"Which you asked me not to do. And which I'm not doing. So I repeat. What the fuck?"

"What's the question exactly?" her visitor asks.

"The *question* is *what the fuck?*"

"I'm not really sure how to respond," the woman answers. "Perhaps my name will do. I'm Lilliane. And once you've calmed down a little, I'll show you something else that will also make you curse a lot. I can't wait, honestly."

Lilliane extends her hand. Laney refuses to take it, refuses to move an inch from where her feet are planted just inside the doorway to her dorm room.

"We're on the seventh floor," Laney says. "How did you—?"

"What the fuck?" Lilliane finishes for her.

"Yeah."

"Laney Foley, we can do this one of two ways. I can show you a variety of things I'm capable of, none of which you will ever be able to explain in any rational or scientific way. And a great many of which will reduce you to a sputtering wreck in the corner of your room. *Or* I can show you only those things that you will eventually be able to dismiss and discount once I'm on my way. Option two, I can assure you, will allow you to lead a far more balanced and normal life. And believe it or not, despite the manner in which I have entered it, my objective is for you to lead a balanced and normal life from here on out."

"There's nothing normal about jumping seven stories through an open window."

"It wasn't open. But yes, you're right. There's nothing normal about it. Just as there is nothing normal about this candle."

The candle in question is still on Laney's desk, right next to her open laptop, easily within Lilliane's reach, but the older woman refuses to touch it. Instead, she studies it as if it were a dead rat.

"Have you calmed down a bit or do you need to curse some more?" Lilliane asks.

"I'm done cursing. For now."

"Good. Then read the webpage I've opened on your computer."

At her desk, Laney tilts the monitor back until the sun isn't whiting out the screen. When she hits the right angle, she finds herself staring down at a black and white photograph of Lilliane. Her hair is different, and the posed, black-and-white photo looks like it's from another era, but it's definitely the same woman. The site is called *FORGOTTEN INJUSTICE*, its title framed by ghostly human profiles with no facial features. Laney scans the captions above and below Lilliane's picture, then clicks on some of the links in the header to make sure the site is legit. On another page, she comes across a recent *Times Picayune* article praising the site's mission, which is to document old, unsolved missing persons cases within the black community local newspapers refused to report on at the time. The woman standing right behind her is one of those cases. And she hasn't aged a day since she went missing.

And there it is, Laney thinks. One day, you're walking along and then suddenly something totally inexplicable drops right down in the middle of your life. Either you lose your mind or this extraordinary thing—a woman who hasn't aged a day in fifty-six years, for instance—becomes as undeniable as gravity. After all, wasn't there a time in all of our lives when complete sentences sounded to us like magic because we couldn't yet speak one ourselves? How was this any different? How is the woman and what she might be capable of any different to Laney's everyday life than a complete sentence is to an infant?

"This is you," Laney hears herself say.

"Yes."

"This is you in nineteen fifty-nine."

"That is me, four months before I met Bastian Drake."

"I see." *No, I don't.*

"Do you need to curse again?"

"Maybe."

"It doesn't offend me. It's a sign that you're not focused and I would like you to be able to retain everything I'm about to say to you."

"Okay. *Fuck*. There, I said it. It's out of my system."

Laney sinks down into her desk chair. It occurs to her, too late, that Lilliane now stands between her and her only exit. But there's nothing menacing in the woman's expression. She looks sheepish, and after a few seconds, she manages an indulgent smile.

"He's a ghost," Lilliane finally says.

"A ghost? Bastian Drake is a ghost?"

"Yes. Last night you had an extended conversation with and accepted a gift from a ghost. Just as in April of nineteen fifty-nine I wandered into a strange little candle shop in the French Quarter I'd never seen before and had an extended conversation with *and* accepted a gift from a ghost."

"Am I dead right now?" Laney asks.

"No. Focus. What did it smell like?"

"Bastian?"

"The candle."

"Vanilla. Vanilla and campfires."

"And I take it the man for whom you have deep feelings smells exactly the same way?"

"Yes," Laney whispers.

Lilliane smiles distantly, nostalgically, and for a second Laney thinks her visitor is blinking back tears. But none come. Maybe this woman, this *being*, isn't capable of making them.

"Mine was pears and cinnamon," Lilliane says. "Pears and cinnamon," she adds, her voice a hoarse whisper.

"Are you a ghost too?" Laney asks.

"No. Changed, yes. But not a ghost."

"Changed by what? By Bastian?"

"Close. By his candle. By *that* candle," she says, pointing to the one next to Laney's elbow. "His shop. It never appears in the same place twice, you see. And it only appears to someone like you, someone struggling with what they want and how they want it. *Bastian* only appears to someone like you, I should say, and he only gives a candle to someone suffering under the same struggle."

"And you were suffering?" Laney asks, and then forces herself to gulp before she says, "In nineteen fifty-nine?"

Lilliane closes her eyes, shakes her head as if shrugging off the memory.

"He'll tell you that most of the time his magic, the magic in that candle, only does good. That once lit, the flame releases a force that allows a person's true passion to become their everyday life. And how can that be a bad thing?"

"And what would *you* tell me about his magic?"

"That there is a risk to it," Lilliane says. "A risk he doesn't disclose. I would tell you there are some people in whom fear runs so deep, in whom resistance is so strong, the flame's energy isn't strong enough to overpower them."

"Wait a minute," Laney says. "Just tell me, if I were to light this candle right now, what would happen? What would I see?"

"You would see something that would either make you scream bloody murder or fall down on your knees in prayer. Or possibly both. And then, shortly thereafter, you would have the most intense orgasm of your entire life. Then you would regain consciousness covered in a kind of gold residue which you wouldn't be able to wipe off or shower away, and you would go to the man you currently desire with absolute surrender and abandon and a total absence of fear."

Neither one of them speaks for several minutes. Outside, a bird chirps madly. Is it trying to warn her the woman she's talking to just flew seven stories up the side of Berry Hall?

"And you *don't* want me to light this candle?" Laney finally asks.

"What I've just described is one possible scenario. There are two. If you're one of the obstinate ones, like I was, if your mind is strong enough to talk yourself out of your desire, even when that desire is amplified by the flame's energy, things will go very differently."

"Okay…"

"Are you a stubborn person, Laney Foley? Are you full of reasons why it will never work with the man you can't chase from your thoughts and your heart?"

Her answer is in the speed with which her eyes drop to the pockmarked linoleum floor between them.

"I see," Lilliane whispers. "It's a good thing I warned you then."

"And what happens to the stubborn ones?" Laney asks. "What happened to you?"

"We call ourselves Radiants. It's far better than what he used to call us."

"Bastian?"

"Yes. *The Refused.* That was his nickname for us in the beginning. Because we had refused his gift, you see."

"How?"

"The flame's energy is drawn from those who have lived out their deepest sexual desires. That's what fuels his candles. The life force of desire, if you will. Bastian used to collect this force himself. I'm not exactly sure how. There's much he won't tell me. Now I collect it for him, at a place I run called The Desire Exchange."

Amazing that the name of a silly urban legend seems like the only *real* thing in this entire conversation. Maybe because it's familiar.

"I always thought that place was a joke," Laney says.

"Everyone does. It's how we stay exclusive."

"You run it?"

"Yes. It's where I've managed to put some of my abilities to use. To *good* use, that is. I was the first, you see. The first person to refuse his gift."

"But, Lilliane, what does that mean, to refuse his gift? I don't understand."

"It means that for twenty-four hours after you light the candle, twenty-four hours after you see spirits emerge from it and you're bathed in an energy that fills you with a desire like you have never known, even then, you *still* don't go to the person you desire with all your heart. You don't complete the connection the flame is driving you to make. And so, the flame's energy never reaches its final destination. It becomes trapped within you and as a result you are forever changed."

"How?"

Lilliane looks into Laney's eyes for the first time in several minutes, and while she's yet to shed a tear, the pain is so raw and evident it's hard for Laney to hold the woman's gaze. But it would be too rude to look away.

"I don't want to say," Lilliane says.

"Why?"

"Because it will sound better than it is. And I don't wish my life for you. For anyone."

"Don't I have the right to make a choice?" Laney asks. "Isn't that why you came? So that I could know the risk?"

"I've stayed out of Bastian's affairs until now. But I wasn't prepared for how I'd feel when I saw it all again. When I saw you standing there just like me. The shop exactly like it was all those years ago, just on a different street."

"You think I'll want to be like you if you tell me what you are?"

"Perhaps."

"If all you wanted was to keep me from lighting this candle, why didn't you just jump back out the window with it before I got upstairs?"

"I don't know," she answers. It sounds almost petulant.

"Of course you do. You waited. You waited to tell me all of this. So don't just give me half your story. Please."

The woman takes a seat on Laney's bed, her posture as casual as a friend who just dropped by for a chat and Diet Coke. The forced nature of this gesture chills Laney to the bone.

"I don't age, as you can see from that picture. I don't sleep, because I don't need to. I don't eat. And I don't fly, exactly. But I leap, which is sort of like flying but you can't let the mind wander for very long." Then, as if she's just rattled off the items on a grocery list, she smooths her dress over her thighs and offers Laney a weak smile.

"Is that all?" Laney asks in a hoarse, strained voice.

"No," Lilliane says primly. "If I suck in a little bit of your breath, I have the power to make your deepest sexual fantasy materialize in your immediate physical area for an extended period of time. To do this, I literally dematerialize."

"Dematerialize?"

"I cease to exist as an individual being on this physical plane. I become your fantasy. All of it. The room, the props, the players. It's another fun perk of the energy that's been trapped in me for fifty-six years."

"I see."

"No, you don't. And it's my hope that you never will."

"Because you think if you just tell me about this stuff and don't show any of it to me, I'll be able to pretend like none of this ever happened once you leave."

"Once I leave *with* the candle. Yes."

"You can't just wipe my memory or something?"

"No. I cannot."

"Good, I guess," Laney says. "So the energy in this candle, you collect it for him even though you know the risk, even though it turned you into something amazing you don't want to be?"

Lilliane averts her eyes. "There was no one else like me in the beginning. Bastian was all I had. And even he wasn't sure what had happened to me. We figured it out together as best we could. And then a few years later, there was another. And another. And we saw the trend. By then, I'd become comfortable with my new abilities so I took over some of his operations. I thought it would allow me to control him. But there's no controlling him. He can't even control himself."

"How come?"

Lilliane meets Laney's stare again. "He's a servant to forces he doesn't fully understand. But if you must know, I help people at The Desire Exchange. They leave enlightened, not *transformed.* And by God, I help far more people than he appears to on the streets of the French Quarter. That's for sure. It's good work I do."

"And ten bucks says it's got something to do with your other power. The one where you…" Laney can't even bring herself to repeat the words Lilliane just used. *Dematerialize*? Become a fantasy? It's all nuts! "So is that all?" Laney asks.

"All of what?"

"All of how you've been changed."

"No," Lilliane says, shaking her head, staring into Laney's eyes again with a piercing look that threatens to break Laney's heart. And then the piercing look is joined by a dazzling gold radiance that fills both of the woman's eye sockets, a radiance that rides the swell of emotion within Lilliane. It's a full-fledged display of something Laney only glimpsed in Bastian's eyes the night before. Then it's gone and Lilliane once again stares back at her with beautiful, but very human brown eyes, filled with pain, but not with otherworldly golden light.

"I can feel lust," Lilliane says, her voice almost a whisper. "I can feel raw sexual attraction to another person. But I have no desire to commit to them. To anyone. I have never again had the experience of looking at a man and believing that anything would be possible if he just took me in his arms.

"True love, Laney Foley, is wanting the world for someone even when they won't do what you tell them to, even when they don't want you back. True love is the ability to make yourself absolutely vulnerable to someone despite the risks. In fact, when you're truly in love, the only real risk is that you won't do justice to that love. It's a hard thing to define, true love. I'll give you that. But you can define it when it's gone. Oh, my heavens, how you can define it when it's gone. Believe me. *That* is how I have *also* been changed, Laney Foley. And I do not wish the same for you or anyone."

"How do you know, Lilliane? How do you know it's been removed from you completely?"

"I went to him," she whispers. "After several days, after I realized that simply lighting a candle given to me by a strange white man in the French Quarter had changed my fundamental being, I went to the man I smelled every time I lifted that candle to my nose. I went to the man who had once filled my dreams and made my heart flutter every time he came near. And when I looked at him I felt nothing. It was as if I was staring upon sandpaper and dust. I could take to the sky but my heart had been emptied."

"Maybe you were just angry," Laney says. "You'd had a traumatic experience. You probably—"

"I know your intentions are good, Miss Foley, but I've had decades to sort through this. Literally decades. This is my story, I'm sorry to say. The same is true for the other Radiants."

"How many are there?" Laney asks.

"Twenty-three," she answers. "And when I saw you in that shop last night, I was not willing to add another to our ranks."

For a while, neither one of them speaks. A dull pounding of bass echoes down the hall. It's that hushed period of early evening when most classes are finished and students have retreated to their dorm rooms before venturing out to dinner.

Did a part of her innately sense Bastian Drake's shop had some kind of magic to it? The same part of her that might assume a strange, distant sound in a creaky old house could possibly be a ghost. And did she really not care or pause to consider the idea because Bastian *seemed* totally sincere about her well-being?

Is it easier to believe in guardian angels or demons? She's not entirely sure. But she's willing to bet it's the former. Which one is Bastian Drake?

"So," Laney finally says, her voice sounding reedy and distant. "If I light the candle, I'll either be forced to have sex with the man I'm falling for, or I'll freak out and run, and then I'll be turned into an immortal who can never fall in love again. Both options sound like rape, if you ask me."

"You don't have to have sex with him to complete the connection. You simply have to tell him the truth that's in your heart. Whether or not you use your entire body to do it is up to you."

"But that's not what happened to you?"

"As I said, once the other Radiants started to come in, we collected their experiences, identified the trends. Some of them went to the object of their desire right after they lit the flame and had quite a time in between the sheets. But they ran like hell as soon as orgasms were achieved. They never told the person how they truly felt. That's the key."

"That and you have to stay with them for twenty-four hours?" Laney asks.

"No. For a sleep."

"I'm sorry. A what?"

"You have to share yourself with them either physically or verbally and then sleep beside them for a night. Which might have something to do with why Radiants never sleep again."

"And if you stay the night, you stay with them forever?"

"Oh, no. You stay with them for as long as it's meant to last. The flame offers an opportunity to finally act, not a guarantee that it will last forever once you do."

"None of this is fair," Laney mutters.

"Oh, Laney Foley. Find me a world that's fair and I will take you in my arms and fly us to it. The supernatural universe contains as many quirks and rules as quantum physics."

"Yeah, I'm getting that. Provided, you know, you're not nuts."

"This man of yours," Lilliane says. "The one who smells of campfires and vanilla. What's his name?"

"Michael?"

"Is he resisting what exists between you?"

"God, no," Laney answers. "He couldn't be resisting any less."

"Good. Then he'll be safe no matter what you decide."

"What do you mean?"

"Some Radiants start out as the objects of desire for those who light the flame, only they resist it too, because it's terrifying. The energy comes to them and they know nothing of the candle in the first place so—"

"Get it out of here," Laney says. She's on her feet before she realizes she's made the decision to stand. Her back is to her desk, and the candle and the laptop with its screen filled with the vintage photograph of Lilliane. "Take it. Please. Just get it out of here."

"Are you sure?"

"Well, aren't you happy? Isn't this what you wanted?"

"I wanted you to be able to make a choice based on all the infor—"

"I've made it. Take it. Please."

"Very well," Lilliane whispers.

Facing her roommate's side of the room, Laney studies the Keurig coffee maker and the perfectly made bed and all the photographs of

Perfect Skinny Kelley and her perfect family on a variety of beach vacations, hoping these ordinary objects will return to her to a sane and normal world. But even as she tries not to, she's listening intently to the small scraping sounds of Lilliane lifting the candle up off the desk.

"There's something else that I want," Lilliane finally says.

"Lilliane, I don't mean to be rude, but I don't think I can handle any—"

"Go to him," Lilliane says. "Go to him and tell him the truth that's in your heart. You don't need magic or a ghost to help you do it. Find the courage within yourself and go to him as soon as you can. If I am proof of anything, it's that all the time in the world can't bring back certain moments, certain opportunities."

Laney turns to face the woman just as she starts for the door.

"Lilliane!"

Startled, Lilliane turns in the doorway.

"What if he's not happy that I didn't light the candle? Could he appear to me again?"

"That won't happen," Lilliane says with utter confidence.

"How are you so sure?"

"Because I'll make sure it won't."

"Thank you," Laney whispers.

Lilliane nods and starts to leave again.

"And Lilliane?"

The woman stops, but she doesn't return Laney's stare.

"I don't believe you," Laney says before she can think twice.

"Which part?"

"I don't believe you can never fall in love again. I think it's still in you somewhere. Maybe it's just a matter of time."

"And what makes you think that?"

"What you did today was too kind and selfless for me to believe your heart is empty."

Lilliane looks up, giving Laney an answer to her earlier question. Yes, Radiants can cry.

"Thank you, Laney," Lilliane says. "And I wish you and Michael the very best."

With a polite nod that belies her tears, Lilliane departs with the candle in one hand, carrying the scent of Bastian Drake's frightening magic away down the hall.

11

Thirty minutes after Lilliane exited Laney's dorm room, in the traditional, non-flying manner, Laney has walked most of the distance to the restaurant where Michael waited. He sent the address by text while she and Lilliane were discussing ghosts, magic candles, and *dematerialization.*

Lilliane was right about one thing. In no time at all, Laney has started to discount some of the more impossible suggestions of the woman's visit. She's decided the website had to have been a fake, for sure. You could do amazing things with Photoshop, like forge an entire *Times Picayune* article. Or make a photograph you took yesterday afternoon look fifty-six years old.

That flying up the side of a seven-story building, though? See, that *one's harder to—*

They're all members of a cult. That's it. A cult that makes strange drugged candles that sometimes poison people, and Lilliane's crazy tale of flame energy was designed to cover up their criminal enterprise. Laney has a hunch that a good cover story doesn't sound completely and utterly wacko, and also doesn't take almost an hour to tell. But who knows? Maybe Lilliane thought Laney was some paranoid stoner who went for psychic readings every other week and would totally buy into a nutso story of spirits and ghosts and haunted candles and—

Yeah, and then there's the part where she just appeared in your room. On the seventh floor. *Without using the elevator or the stairs. Which meant she had to fly, or leap, or whatever she said she does, up the side of the—*

Michael spots her through the restaurant's glass front door. He's sitting by himself at the mostly empty bar. The place is homey and brightly lit, surrounded by sleepy residential blocks, the exact opposite of the rowdy elegance that surrounded them the night before. The quieter surroundings give her a sense of elation. Laney wonders if she's coming to accept that only moments before she was visited by something, by *someone*, truly extraordinary. If only half of what Lilliane said was true, perhaps anything is possible. It seems the world is more limitless than Laney previously thought. She wants to savor this feeling while it lasts, this sense that the prison of rules and risks Laney has lived in for most of her life was just a sandcastle waiting to crumble under the force of a gentle tide.

Is this how she would have felt if she'd actually lit that damn candle? Fearless and elated?

If she hadn't left her dorm in a daze, she might have remembered to bring her umbrella. Only a light roll or two of thunder interrupted the walk there, but suddenly there's a crack loud enough to make her jump.

A small tinkling bell heralds her arrival when she opens the restaurant's front door. There's no host, just a waitress making friendly conversation with the customers at one of her tables, so no one stops her as she walks toward the empty barstool next to Michael. His smile could melt ice, but the rest of him is poised and rigid. *Tense*. He probably figures a big hug isn't the best move given the last time they saw each other she was running like hell in the opposite direction.

"They have a dessert here that is literally a scoop of ice cream on top of a doughnut," he says without preamble.

"Seriously?"

"I am *so* serious. We didn't have dessert last night, so I figured it would give us something to do."

"Something to do?"

"Yeah, while we wait for the moment of truth."

"What do you mean?"

"Well, I'm not your teacher anymore, so if you just don't like me I guess now's the time to say it so we can part as friends. But I recommend waiting until you've had just a little of this doughnut because it is truly one of the best things on the—"

"Michael Brouchard, I've wanted you from the moment I laid eyes on you."

He looks like the wind's been knocked out of him. Was she really that coy? Did he really have that much doubt about how she felt for him?

She wants to break eye contact so she can hold on to the courage she needs to speak the truth of her heart, but there's no looking away from the suddenly vulnerable expression on his face.

"I knew it the first time I saw you," she continues, "the first time I heard you speak, the first time you shared your heart with your class. I knew I'd never met a man like you and I would never meet a man like you again. And the way I felt for you in that moment scared me so bad I did everything I could to deny it. And I waited. I waited each day for you to screw up and give me some sign you weren't really the man I wanted you to be. And every day I sat there and gazed up into your beautiful eyes, I realized that sometimes—*sometimes* a fantasy comes true. All my life I've wanted to feel for someone the way I feel about you. I just had no idea I'd be so goddamn scared when those feelings finally showed up.

"I tried to rehearse this on the walk over. But all I did was come up with a million ways to tell you how I might screw this up if we *try*. A million ways to tell you I'm less than perfect. Because there's a part of me that thinks if I just lay it out on the table now, you'll be able to forgive me if I run again."

"I've already forgiven you," he says.

"I know. But I don't want to sound like this big victim or an angry poor girl with a shell around her heart. And I don't want to plan my escape. And now I know that's a good thing, that I'm afraid, afraid of the way I feel for you. It's a good thing because it means it's real. It means I'm going to give you something I've never given anyone before."

He pales.

"I'm not a virgin," Laney says quickly. "That's not what I'm talking about."

"Okay," Michael says quietly, sounding relieved. Laney pauses. Michael watches her intently and simply waits.

"I'm giving you my trust," she tells him.

"Trust."

"Yeah. It's not something I give out easily. If you haven't noticed."

She grabs for the nearest napkin. As she uses it to wipe at her tears, she feels Michael gently take her other hand in his.

There's a crack of thunder loud enough to make everyone in the restaurant jump. Outside, a deluge begins, instantly rattling the huge plate glass windows.

"I've noticed," Michael whispers. He brings her fingers to his lips and kisses them gently. "I just figured that would make me feel honored once I finally earned it."

She laughs, which brings more tears to her eyes. As they clear, she feels a stab of embarrassment or shame.

"So you're not a fan of virgins?"

"I'm not looking for a conquest, Laney. There are no notches on my belt."

"That's 'cause you mostly wear braided belts."

"I get a lot of crap for that."

"Not from me. I think they're classy. But mostly I like that you can't leave notches in them. It speaks to your character."

"Does it?" he asks with a broad smile. "Well, I'm glad you noticed."

"Were you just listening? There's almost nothing about you I haven't noticed."

"Likewise. But the point is, I'm looking for a partner, Laney. I'm not looking for a woman who only lets me sketch her one time."

"Good to know," she says, lacing her fingers through his until the two of them are officially and indisputably holding hands.

Thunder cracks, followed by a flash of lightning. Everyone in the restaurant jumps again except for them. They're too busy staring into each other's eyes.

"Do I really need to write in shorter paragraphs?" Laney asks.

"What do I care? I'm not your teacher anymore." He makes his eyebrows dance up and down and gives her an evil grin.

"No, but seriously, the stuff you said last night—"

"Was a lot of *bull*," he says. "I was just trying to prove that I could be objective if I had to stay your teacher."

"Could you?"

"Could I have stayed your teacher?"

"Could you have been objective?" she asks.

"Probably not."

"Well," Laney says, lifting his fingers to her lips, and giving them a gentle kiss. "It's a good thing you're not my teacher anymore."

"I'll say," he whispers.

She gives his fingers another kiss. Just this simple, tender act causes her pulse to quicken.

"I know you don't believe it yet, but you belong here, Laney," he says quietly.

"At this school or with you?"

"Both."

The lightning and thunder return. This time the flash is so bright, for a few seconds it covers up the fact that the power has gone out. The customers inside the restaurant groan as total darkness descends.

"Well," Michael says, gripping her hand and sliding off his stool.

"Looks like we're gonna have to find another place for desert."

"Where's that?"

"We'll figure it out."

Michael didn't bring an umbrella either, so he takes off his leather jacket and holds it over their heads as he guides her in the direction of his car. It's one of those relentless New Orleans storms, the kind that usually blows through on summer afternoons and are twice as frightening when they appear at night, with their fat, pelting drops and sudden gusts of wind. The power is out on the entire street which turns the cars alongside them into vague, dripping shadows. She has no idea which belongs to Michael. When he stops suddenly next to a stubby, bright-orange box with tires, she almost loses her footing.

Once he shuts the door after her, once she's sealed inside the little box, she starts laughing.

"It's a Kia Soul!" she cries as he slides behind the wheel.

"Are you making fun of my car?"

"No. I'm so happy."

"Why? It's not that great, really. And it's used. My friend's loaning it to me until I can afford to get something else 'cause even he hates it."

"Yeah, but it's a Kia Soul. Don't you understand?"

"No!"

He turns the key in the ignition. The first squeal doesn't sound promising.

"All my friends, hell, make that everyone around me, have all this expensive crap all the time. Cat's got a brand new BMW. My roommate's got this Keurig coffee maker and she acts like it's a charity project to let me have four a day. Meanwhile, I can't even afford a smartphone. But *you*. You, Michael Brouchard, drive a crappy *used* Kia Soul, and that is a beautiful, beautiful thing."

"And it won't start," he says.

"Seriously?"

"Seriously," he says. He turns the key again. Nothing happens.

"Oh."

"We could go back inside the restaurant," he offers.

"We could."

"Or we could stay here," he says.

"What would we do if we stayed here?"

Before they have time to speculate, he's curved an arm around her upper back and brought their bodies as close together as he can over the gear shift, close enough for his mouth to find hers, for his free hand to cup the side of her face gently, then her chin, holding her in place so he can direct and focus the force of his kiss.

He is panting when he breaks, lips still inches from hers. "I guess we could stay here and make out like teenagers."

"Or discuss some extra credit," she whispers.

"I'm not your teacher anymore, Miss Foley."

At these words, her waist suddenly feels molten, liquid, a reminder that not only is she free from the risk of damaging her academic standing, *he's* the one who set her free. He's the one who made the effort to switch her to a different class. He didn't lecture her or condescend to her or tell her that her fears were meaningless. Instead, he figured out what they were and did his best to make them disappear.

"Oh, yeah," she says, cupping his chin in her hand. "Then get in the backseat with me and prove it."

Even in the rainy darkness, she can see his eyes widen at this brazen request. She can feel the shudder of lust that moves through his body before she releases the back of his neck. She kicks the door open, blinks against the blast of rain, then she's in the backseat only to find he's beaten her there, which makes her laugh.

"Are you sure?" he asks.

"I wouldn't have said it if I wasn't."

He resumes their previous pose, only without the gearshift between them. Arm curved around her upper back, lips together in another determined kiss.

When he breaks, his left hand is kneading the inside of her thigh with a steady rhythm and a firm pressure that bathes her entire body with heat.

"And how exactly do you want me to prove that I'm not your teacher anymore?" he rasps, lips inches from her own.

Deftly, as if it were nothing, he unsnaps the button on her jeans, begins tracing gentle patterns along the newly exposed skin just above the hem of her panties.

"Why don't you start by doing two of the things you always wanted to do to me in class?" she asks in between breaths.

"Just two?" he asks, gently taking her earlobe between his teeth, suckling it briefly, but loud enough to make a slight smack when he releases it.

"All right, before we come up with how many things I'm gonna let you do right here, you can give me a ballpark figure for all the dirty, no-good things you've wanted to do to me since the semester started."

"Should I leave out the things that are only legal in other countries?"

"Let's leave out other countries altogether."

"Well, it's not that I spent the semester wanting to do specific things to you…"— his fingers dip below her panty line, grazing her folds but avoiding her clit—"It's that I wanted to make you respond certain ways. For instance,"—his fingers start a return trip and this time he's narrowed the space between them so she'll know what's coming—"I wanted to see the expression on your face while I gave you absolute"— his fingers arrive at her clit—"total pleasure."

First he grazes it on both sides, then he circles it several times with his index finger before shifting to the pointer finger and back again. The knowledge that he's intently studying her every move while he tests, probes and massages the seat of her bliss causes the pleasure to intensify to such a point that her breaths stutter. He lifts his fingers to his mouth, savors the taste of her, and goes back to work without stopping his intense study of her every writhe and gasp.

"Do I look like you expected me to?" she asks in between gasps. "While you…"

"Oh, no. You look far more beautiful than I even thought possible." His tongue travels the nape of her neck, as another finger joins the first two in their intensifying assault on her clit. "And you taste better than I could have dreamed."

The rhythm of his tongue against her neck is exploratory and eager; the rhythm of his fingers on her clit is determined and confident. The combination of the two makes her dizzy. His husky whisper is in her ear.

"This is what I'd like to draw. *This.* Right here. *You.* The way you look when I do my hardest to make you moan, to make you come. You, right now, under my touch. You're art in the making, Laney Foley."

The rain veils the windows, and the blacked-out street offers no stray illumination strong enough to pierce the veil. But she still feels deliciously exposed. Wedged together in the cramped backseat, at first their pose seemed forced and awkward. But now, Michael's half embrace feels all-consuming. His choice to keep one arm curved around her upper back doesn't just steady her as jolts of pleasure shoot through her, it reminds her that he isn't clawing at her in a desperate bid to secure his own release. He has devoted himself utterly and entirely to her pleasure, and that alone deserves some kind of reward.

When she moves to free him, he starts to dazzle her clit with three dancing fingers, as if he's trying to incapacitate her with pleasure before she has a chance to release his cock. Maybe he relishes the power and the control. But she's determined, and when she finally closes her hand around it, he groans against her neck.

"Laney," he moans, all pretense of student-teacher role-play gone. Her name issues from him on another shuddering groan as her hand slides the considerable length of his erect cock. "*Laney…*"

"This is one of the things *I've* wanted to do all semester," she whispers.

Just one? She expects him to ask. But he's past the point of dirty talk. Instead, he lifts the fingers he's been probing her with to his lips again, sucks her juices from his fingertips, teeth clenching, breath leaving him in a hiss at the raw taste of her.

"Laney…" He groans again.

She's amazed and delighted that a backseat make-out session could blossom into this flowering of desire. She's dizzy over the realization that simply by pleasuring her, Michael brought himself so close to release that the head of his cock is flame-hot and throbbing in her grip. And this thought brings her to the edge of bliss as well. The sight of her, every facial expression during this delicious assault, tasting her on his fingertips—all of these things have stripped quick words and any trace of restraint from the man of her dreams. She feels like a goddess of infinite power.

"Laney," he cries. There's an almost desperate tone to his voice. Someone outside of the car might have been able to hear him, she isn't sure. The rain is still drumming against the roof and windows, but his fingers are still working a frenzied rhythm against her clit, which turns all of her worries about the outside world into something as light and easily lifted as a wedding veil.

When she's confident he's within seconds of release, she says, "Michael?"

He stares into her eyes, but he's too breathless to answer with words.

"This is what I want to see," she whispers.

He tries to kiss her, but his orgasm rips through him before his lips can make it to hers. For a few seconds his mouth is a silent O, until the rapid-fire groans tear from him like desire's gunfire. To witness his orgasm from this close, their noses inches apart, his hot gasps bathing her lips, causes her scalp to tighten and that special spot in between her shoulder blades to tingle. Her hand is slick with his cum and her strokes have spread it down the length of his shaft.

Michael collapses against one side of her body, breathing against her neck. She figures he's spent. His fingers have stopped their blessed work on her pussy. He's now caressing her mound in lazy, inattentive circles with the heel of his palm, too exhausted to probe it but still to hungry to let it go.

But then suddenly, he's shifting beside her. Sitting up, moving around, moving *her*. Before she realizes quite what's happening, he's pulled off her jeans, spread her down the length of the seat, her upper back resting against the door as his sweaty palms spread her thighs. Even spent and covered in his own cum, he's still devoted to her pleasure. She's just spotted the crown of his head through the shadows above her waist when his teeth graze her clit and he applies a sucking pressure with both lips that makes her feet feel like they're about to float free from her body.

She's close to the edge, feels the promise of a thundering orgasm building like approaching storm clouds. But she can feel resistance too, and with it, the sudden fear that she's separating from her body, that her fear is taking over again. He's working frenzied magic on her sex, but she needs more than his fingers and his tongue. She needs *him*.

"Up," she manages.

"What?" he gasps. His wide eyes stare up her prone body, his jaw slathered in her juices.

"With me," she manages, gasping. "Up here with me—*be* with me."

He gets the message. Michael slides up the backseat, lips suddenly within inches of hers, arm curving under her back, his weight and his power blanketing her suddenly, making her feel both prone, exposed but also protected, all in the same delirious moment. She can tell he's hesitant to give her a taste of her most secret parts, so she grabs his chin and brings their mouths together, and he takes this as a signal to drive the heel of his palm gently against her nub, before the tips of his middle two fingers take up a slow, steady, measured walk atop her throbbing clit.

Exposed, but protected. Probed, but held. These combinations make the specifics of their location—crammed in the backseat of a stranded car on a darkened street in a rainstorm—seem like vague abstractions. Suddenly anything beyond the feel of his fingers against her, the taste of his tongue and the low breathy growls as he seeks to drive her over the edge of bliss cease to exist. Suddenly there is only him. And that's when her pure pleasure takes the form of a scream that could be mistaken for terror by someone who hadn't just discovered what every inch of her tasted like. She expects him to close a hand over her mouth, to muffle her cries. But instead, he grinds his nose against the nape of her neck and laughs encouragingly, gently and with a sound of such rich satisfaction she wishes she could bottle it and save it forever.

When her sense of times returns, she's still shuddering.

"I can't move," Michael finally says. He's still right where he landed as her orgasm tore through her, on top of her and pinning her to the seat, his lips pressed to the nape of her neck.

"Me either," she says.

"I don't want to move."

"Me either."

"Let's not move."

"Sounds like a plan," she says, stroking the back of his neck. "Or maybe just to the side. A little bit. So I can breathe again."

"Sure," he says, following her instruction.

It works. When they were lying in a cramped tangle, bathed in the afterglow of their frenzied climax, she couldn't have cared less about breathing normally. All that mattered was the weight of him and his determination not to let her go, and she wouldn't have said anything to disrupt it. But if they're going to talk, oxygen is key.

Neither one of them has pulled up their underwear or buttoned their jeans, and as they lie together across the backseat, their exposed privates rest against each other, still pulsing heat.

"What are we going to do about your car?" Laney asks.

"Wait until the rain stops and see if someone from the restaurant will give us a jump," he says. "I'm not in any rush, are you?"

"Hell, no. We've waited this long."

"I probably shouldn't say this now, but I would have waited longer if you'd asked me to."

"And that's why I didn't want to make you wait another day," she answers.

"So what happened?" Michael asks her.

The rain hasn't let up in the slightest and the power in the surrounding neighborhood isn't back on. But they've managed to arrange themselves in a comfortable, intimate tangle in the Kia's cramped backseat, and right now, Laney wouldn't trade these cramped quarters for a beach lounger in the south of France.

"I mean, I know I give good e-mail, but it wasn't *that* good," he says. "Or was it? I feel like something else happened, something that made you change your mind. Or your heart."

A change of heart. That's one way of putting it.

Too bad she can't think of any normal, everyday terms to describes Lilliane's visit. Michael seems to feel these thoughts moving through her and props himself up, smoothing her hair away from her face.

"Was it not being your teacher anymore that did it?" he asks.

"Sort of."

"Sort of?" he asks. "Seriously. What happened?"

The same resistance that knotted itself through her muscles the night before when he kissed her in Jackson Square returns. But this time she feels justified. If she tells him anything about Bastian or Lilliane, he'll think she's a lunatic. But another voice joins the chorus of fear in her head, and this one sounds more steady and clear. What happened today *happened*, the voice tells her. There's no way around it, and if she doesn't tell Michael about it, it's as good as keeping a secret. And is that really how she wants to cap off a night of total honesty and total bliss?

There will always be a reason not to tell her truth. There will always be a reason not to bare her heart. There will always be the fear that she is too poor, too angry, too blunt, too smart for her own good. Fear, she has learned, will latch on to any self-doubt or insecurity you have in its quest to keep your life small. Fear tells you it's protecting your heart when it's really just starving it to death.

"Laney?" Michael asks into the sudden, growing silence between them.

"Do you believe in ghosts?"

She can sense a smart remark on the tip of his tongue. But the seriousness in her tone takes a second to wash over him. He grunts before answering. "I'm—well, I guess I'm willing to believe in a lot of things, if someone gives me proof, yeah."

"Okay. A few things first."

"Sure."

"First I need to say I'm not on any drugs, legal or illegal. I have no history of mental illness, although I'm probably a good candidate for anxiety disorder."

"Many of us are," Michael says gently.

Michael sits up suddenly, then gently pulls her to a seated position next to him and begins tugging her jeans up partway. She does the rest of the work of covering herself, allowing him to do the same for himself. Then, just when she thinks she's going to have to tell this story with the two of them awkwardly sitting side by side in the backseat, he leans against the door next to him and invites her to wilt into his body, a small gesture that makes what she's about to do feel much easier.

"Okay," she continues, "and I want you to know, I'm just telling you what I saw and what I heard. I still don't know what any of it means."

"You can tell me whatever you need to tell me, Laney," he says.

And she does. Starting with the moment she ran from him the night before, she takes Michael through her visit to Bastian Drake's shop, describing the candle, its smell—*his* smell—the notecard and her strange but inspiring conversation with Bastian. Next, she describes Lilliane's visit, complete with its stalkery opening act, doing her best to leave nothing out, which isn't easy. Every now and then she has to circle back to fill in some detail of Lilliane's crazy story she left out the first time. All the while, Michael remains silent, listening to her intently as rain drums the roof.

By the time she's finished, the afterglow of their first shared orgasm is gone.

She prepares herself for an interrogation spiced with accusations.

"You're safe?" he asks, but it takes her a second or two to realize it's a question. "This woman, Lilliane. Whoever she is, she assured you that you're safe from whoever these people are, right?"

"I love that that's your first question."

"Of course it is," he says, and kisses her forehead. "Why wouldn't it be?"

"Well, you could have gone with, *Are you fucking nuts*?"

"Someone else could have gone with that. Not me."

"Someone like my father, you mean?"

"That's not my place to say. Yet."

"You did just go down on me, remember?"

"Like I'd ever forget, Miss Foley," he whispers, tracing the edge of her chin gently with one finger, as gently as he traced patterns along the bare flesh of her stomach before he explored her pussy for the first time. It's true that she'd asked him not to call her Miss Foley. But that was a different time, a different time only twenty-four hours in the past, but it still felt like a dark and remote period of her life—a *before* time when the fear that he'd never taste the most intimate parts of her dogged her every step. Now that he's not her teacher anymore, any role-play to the effect will send gooseflesh up the insides of her thighs.

"Let me guess," she says. "Your parents are perfect. Your mom sends you baked goods and your dad welcomes you home with a box of cigars and man talk around the fireplace."

"My parents are perfect at sending checks and asking me when I'm going to get some sense and apply to law school. But I'm not complaining. The checks are big, but I put as much of them as I can in savings. As for the *man talk* around the fireplace, ever since my father retired three years ago, they've spent a grand total of five minutes in the continental United States. I think it's better that way."

"Do they come home for holidays at least?" Laney asks.

"Nope."

"Not even Christmas?"

"Not even Flag Day," he says with an arch smile that does little to hide his bitterness. "It's better that way. Trust me."

"Why?"

"Because then I only have to justify the meaning of the creative arts to my students."

"How'd you turn out so civilized?"

The question throws him. He studies her through the darkness, brushes her hair again from the side of her face. "*They're* civilized, I guess," he finally says, sounding distant, as if he's still measuring his answer.

"Sorry," Laney says, taking his hand. She brings his fingers to her lips so she can kiss them gently. "How'd you turn out so—warm, generous, and attentive? So selfless."

Each new term of praise causes his smile to brighten. Either that or each of the tiny kisses she's landed on his fingertips traveled a direct line to his soul. "Sometimes," he says quietly, "the best way to make up for what we weren't given is to give it to someone else."

"Well," Laney says. "I don't do one-way relationships, so expect plenty of it in return."

"Count on it," he whispers, kissing her forehead. "So you've told me what you saw, and I believe every word, but what do *you* think it means?"

"I think there's no logical explanation for how she got up to my room so fast," she says.

"There's not a fire stairway or anything?"

"There's only one and I was on it," Laney says.

"Another entrance maybe?"

"There's the key card entrance, which I went through, and then the fire stairway, which I was on. Now it has an exit door that only opens to the outside, but even if someone propped it open, I was on those stairs the whole time. I would have seen her. And after I walked away from her outside the dorm, she just vanished. She would have had to get between me and one of those doors and she didn't… I mean, the rest of it could just be some crazy woman's rambling. But that part—I just can't get past that part, Michael."

"The things she said, though. Did you believe her?"

"There were moments. There were moments when I believed because she clearly believed it."

"Wow," he says softly.

"I'm sorry, Michael."

"Why are you sorry?"

"This crazy story. This doesn't make for the best start. For us."

He shifts slightly until he can take her face in his hands.

"Are you out of your mind?" he asks in a whisper.

"That's what I was afraid you would say."

"No no no. That's not it."

"Well, then what? I'm so confused."

"If there was even a moment when you believed the things Lilliane said to you today, that means you chose me over the chance to live forever, the chance to be as beautiful as you are now for all time. Tell me, Laney. How could I ask for a better start than that?"

When their lips meet, she takes his face in her hands, enjoys once again the thrill of being able to touch him in such an intimate way. Even though just she's felt the heft of his cock and the heat of his seed. She lays her fingers gently against the hard ridges of his cheekbones and jawline while their kiss seals them together. It still feels as tender and powerful as it did the night before.

12

LILLIANE

Alone on a bench across from St. Louis Cathedral, Lilliane watches the rain collect atop the candle's round bed of wax, marveling at how the deepening pool inside the glass container makes the candle look like a pathetic, ordinary thing. The thunderstorm has cleared Jackson Square of its street musicians and artists. She has set the candle just outside the shelter offered by her umbrella.

It wasn't easy to leave the comfort and warmth of her hotel suite in this storm, but she didn't want to risk Bastian appearing to her at her hotel for the first time. The Montelone has been her safe space for years. But if ever there was a night for Bastian to break decorum and cross a boundary unannounced, it was tonight, on the eve of her thwarting his efforts directly for the first time since they met decades before.

The sudden ghostly silence that fills Jackson Square doesn't surprise her in the slightest. Lilliane has seen Bastian stop time before but the sight this time is impressive. Frozen raindrops surround her, each one suspended perfectly in place. The security lights along the rooflines of the Cabildo and the Presbytere, which seemed to waver only seconds before in the wind and rain, now pierce the air around her, as substantial as ivory tusks. Where their beams hit the frozen raindrops, they carve stained-glass patterns of light and dark through the air itself.

In contrast to the drama of this dramatic, frozen tableaux, Bastian's approaching footsteps are quiet, almost polite. They're the only two people for blocks who can see each other right now. Still, she refuses to look at him as he closes his purple umbrella and rests it against the edge of her bench. She does the same with her own umbrella as he hefts the candle from the bench in both hands.

A sound like a snake's hiss draws her full attention at last.

What was once Bastian's gift for Laney Foley is now dark sand passing through the gaps between his pale, smooth fingers, dark sand laced with just the slightest hints of gold radiance, which flicker and die as it floats through the air, turning to dust, vanishing altogether before it can reach the flagstones at Bastian's feet.

"Never seen that before," Lilliane says.

"Neither have I," Bastian responds.

"Well, there's plenty more where that came from. I've kept you well stocked."

"What will it matter if you try to stop me every time?"

"Oh, Bastian. There's no stopping you."

"You did today."

"Who knows? Maybe today was a one-time thing. Or maybe I'll try again. Depending on my mood."

"Until—?"

"Until what?"

"Is this a game you're going to play with me now?" he asks.

"Are you suggesting I'm trying to blackmail some answers out of you?" Lilliane asks.

"Your words, not mine."

"I see."

"I could just abandon you," he says.

"Could you, really?" she asks. "*Could* you just abandon me, Bastian?"

He doesn't answer.

"That's what I thought," she says. "You have no control over what you do. I saw it last night on the roof of the cathedral. You were pulled away from me by a force you barely understand."

She realizes he is the closest to anger she's ever seen him, and this satisfies her deeply. His eyes are ablaze with the gold radiance they must both work to conceal from ordinary humans in moments of anger and passion.

"Twelve-hundred people," he says.

"Excuse me?"

"Twelve-hundred. That's how many I've visited since this journey began. That's how many I have helped. There are only twenty-three of you, Lilliane."

"Yes, but we live forever with the knowledge of what you've done."

"With what you *failed* to do."

"You liar!" she roars. She's on her feet before she can stop herself, her voice echoing queerly through a square emptied of time and wind. "I was *not* some little college girl with doubt and mixed feelings. He was my boss's son and he was *white*. We could have been lynched, Bastian. What would your *candle* have done for us then?"

"We'll never know," he answers.

"You smug bastard. Sitting in judgment of me when we know nothing of what you really are! You act like a guardian angel, but this is your punishment, isn't it? You and your little shop. You've been sentenced to appear, again and again, at the beck and call of—you don't even *know* what, do you? What I want to know is *why*? What secret are you hiding? What did you do when you were alive to earn this punishment?"

"You have had fifty-six years to be rid of your anger, Lilliane," he growls. "And yet here it is again. Maybe this is all *your* punishment."

"What is your name, Bastian?"

"Good evening, Lilliane."

"What is your *real* name?"

"If there are consequences for what you've done, we shall experience them together, I am sure."

"What is your name?"

In an instant, she is soaked. The rain slams to the flagstones around her. The lights along the roofline overhead take on their indistinct, wavering quality. Time is returned to its normal course and flow. Bastian is gone.

The candle is gone too, reduced to handfuls of vanishing dust in a moment somewhere between the seconds of ordinary mortal time.

Small victories, Lilliane thinks. *Small victories.*

13

LANEY

From the moment she met him, Laney pictured Michael living in a brightly painted shotgun house somewhere near campus, with a small front yard full of strange modern sculptures and a Golden Retriever he'd named after a famous painter. In reality, his tiny studio apartment is in a large, red brick building in the Warehouse District, and there's no trace of a pet. And there are no sculptures, unless you count the elaborate cast-iron frame of his king-sized bed, its posts shaped like obelisks with small, four-sided glass lanterns on top. As she scrapes her muddy shoes on the welcome mat, Michael pulls a box of matches from the nightstand drawer and starts lighting the stubby candles inside each lantern.

The power's working just fine, but he's not turning on any of the lights. Maybe it's a nod to Lilliane's crazy story. Or maybe he's just trying to rush her into bed so he can do all the things to her body they didn't have room for in the Kia's cramped back seat. It didn't take more than fifteen minutes for the temperature inside the stranded car to become stifling, but the rain was still coming down in sheets, so a jump was out of the question. The cab driver was friendly and Laney couldn't help but wonder if the poor guy smelled the scent of sex wafting off his two passengers. Worse, had he been able to detect Laney's struggle not to paw at Michael's cock through his soaked jeans? Now that she has Michael all to herself again, the idea of more delayed gratification feels as delicious as his bed looks.

"A friend of mine's a sculptor," he says. "She made this for me. They're modeled after the lamp posts that light the entrance to St. Peter's Square in Rome."

"Italy," Laney says. But what she's really thinking is, *a* woman *made this bed for you? This whole bed? Who? I'll have Cat investigate. And kill her.* "You love Italy."

"You remembered," he says with a smile.

Don't ask what kind of lady friend would make him a huge, elaborate bedframe out of cast iron. Artists are different. Maybe they make huge expensive things for one another without expecting sex in return.

"Janine," Michael says suddenly.

"Excuse me?"

"She made the bed. Janine. That's her name. And this summer she married her girlfriend in Provincetown."

"So that would mean her girlfriend is now her wife," Laney says.

"Very smart, Miss Foley."

"You're gonna have to stop calling me that, Professor Brouchard."

"Not when it almost makes you come every time I do."

"You know how to make me come for real now. Who cares about making me *almost* come?"

Before he can finish his lustful growl, and before he can close the distance between them, she says, "So is Italy your first real love?"

"You could say that," he says. He curves his arms around her from behind, nuzzles his lips against her neck, allows her to study the bed before them, maybe so she can imagine all the pleasures he'll provide once they're both tangled in its chocolate-colored sheets. Safe from the rain. Safe from the fallout of a teacher-student relationship that might have damaged them both.

"Sophomore year of high school my parents took me on a summer trip to Rome, Florence, and Venice," Michael says, his voice dreamily trailing off. "Let's just say there was my life before I saw the ceiling of the Sistine Chapel and there was my life after. That was the day art became the only way of trying to make sense of the world that held any logic to me. And the whole time, my parents thought I was just weeping because I was exhausted from jet lag."

It feels like this is just Michael talking, not Michael the teacher. He never offered her classmates access to his teenage self, a privileged high school student with a heart so open he wept at his first up-close glimpse of Michelangelo's most famous work even though he was raised by two people with hundred dollar bills and ice water flowing through their veins. For now, this Michael is just for her.

"Want to know what else makes me smart?" Laney asks.

"There's plenty that makes you smart."

"Well, thank you for saying so, but right now I'm smart enough to know you haven't turned on any of the lights, which means there's something in this apartment you don't want me to see."

"*Or,*" he says, kissing her neck softly. "I'm just trying to get in your pants again. I mean, last time I had to cut off power to a whole neighborhood before you let me taste that sweet beautiful little pussy you've got between your legs."

She's not sure if it's the sudden burst of dirty talk or the fact that he delivered it in the same gentle tone of voice with which he told the story of his high school trip to Rome that causes her breath to leave her. His hands slide down her waist. When he cups her thighs, she slips quickly from his embrace, makes a beeline for the side of the apartment he's deliberately left in shadow.

There's a few seconds of fumbling before she finds the switch on a gooseneck lamp. With one flick of her wrist she's illuminated a cramped but orderly art studio. The lamp's bulb is so bright she has to blink for a few seconds to get her bearings.

Two easels flank a drafting table serviced by a high stool. On one of the easels sits the beginnings of an oil painting that looks like a landscape. It could be an abstract; she's not sure. Most of the space is dedicated to larger versions of pencil sketches like the one he gave her the night before. If this were one of those scary movies her friends in high school always wanted her to sneak into, all the drawings on display would be of her. And there would be too many of them and they would all have been drawn from photographs of her he snapped in secret. And the character who played her in the movie would be sort of getting the message that her new lover was a psycho while the girls in the back row of the theatre screamed that very message at the top of their lungs.

But this isn't a horror movie, so she's not the subject of the drawings on display here in Michael's apartment. They are, however, just as detailed and beautiful as the one he presented her with the night before—French Quarter street scenes, images of the riverfront, various angles on the Chamberland University campus. In fact, there's only one or two human figures in any of them, mostly shadowy, distant pedestrians, and that makes the portrait Michael drew of her seem all the more special.

"So is this your secret?" she asks. "You're an actual artist and not just someone who studies them?"

"My secret is that I'm just as happy teaching art as I am making it. Which is a very rare thing indeed. And to be honest, it's not really a secret. A blessing, perhaps."

"So you really *were* just trying to rush me into bed?" she asks.

He's embracing her from behind again, his every touch making her remember the mad, yet focused flicker of his tongue across her clit. At the sight of the dry paintbrushes sitting bristles-up inside an old coffee can, a plan occurs to her.

"Maybe I just thought you'd be a little kinder on my work if you saw it after I made love to you," Michael whispers.

"*Love*, huh?"

"I said I was going to *make* love. I didn't say you'd *fall* in love with me." He gives her a light nip on her earlobe. "Yet."

She clasps his erection through his rain soaked jeans.

"That is *so* inappropriate, Mister Brouchard," she says, tone full of mock indignation.

"Why? I'm not your teacher anymore, *Miss* Foley."

"But you were," she rasps, palming his length as he flickers his tongue against the nape of her neck. "You *were* my teacher, see? And you made me want you more and more every day I came to class. You kept rolling up the sleeves of your shirts so I could see these forearms." She clutches both for effect, as if she were about to pull them free of her waist. She does nothing of the kind. "Some people would call that an abuse of power, Professor Brouchard. Toying with your students like that."

"If you were in my head, *Miss* Foley, seeing the things I saw every time you walked into my classroom, listening to my heart race when you sat down in your desk, you'd know who really had the power." He gives the front of her jeans a hard tug, just hard enough to send a brief shockwave of pleasure through her aching folds.

"Still," she gasps, "some people would say it was wrong. The way you felt about me. The way I feel about you."

"Oh, yeah," he growls into her ear. She hasn't yet heard his voice drop to quite this timbre of raw lust. The sound of it has her soaked. "Should I force those *people* to sit in the corner and watch while I turn your writhing body into a work of art, while I fuck you until you can barely speak? Then those *people* can decide whether or not I did a good enough job of teaching Miss Laney Foley about art."

This isn't just dirty talk. This is delicious, riotously *filthy* talk, and it's threatening to drive her to the bed right then and there.

The plan. The plan. Don't forget your plan!

If it works, she'll have Cat to thank. Who else?

Cat was the one who pulled that silly article from the pages of *Cosmo* a few weeks ago, the one with the picture of the happy couple in bed, smiling as they studied crude pencil sketches of a man and a woman's body. *Your Lover's Special Spots*, it was titled. As Cat read her the article, Laney mocked the idea of drawing circles on some silly sketch just so you could let your lover know where you wanted them to lick you and pinch you and kiss you and probe you. But secretly, behind the sarcasm, she'd longed to have a man do it. And now she had him. But they weren't going to draw on some stupid sketch. She has a much better canvas in mind.

Michael's hard, hungry kiss makes her feet feel like they're leaving the floor. She breaks suddenly, takes a step back and lifts a single admonishing finger into the sudden space between them.

"Not so fast, Professor," she says.

His eyebrows arch. His half-smile is indulgent, but there's a flicker of real fear in it, which is exactly what she was hoping for.

"The power deferential between a teacher and a student can be very, very damaging to intimate relationships like the one you seem *determined* to have with me."

"Is that so?" he asks.

"It *is* so," she says, brushing past him. "It is most certainly so, *Mister* Brouchard. Just ask one of the counselors at the Student Health Center. They even have pamphlets on the subject."

"And I take it you've read every—"

"I'm not *finished*," she snaps. For now, she is the teacher and he is the student. What better way to vent all the stress and pressure of their previously bottled up attractions for one another? Well, there's probably five or six or maybe even eight better ways. But they'll get to those soon enough.

"There are, however, certain *steps* we can take to try to correct that difference," she explains in her best schoolmarm tone. "Make the playing field a little more even, if you will."

"Oh, I will," he says under his breath.

"Focus, Professor."

"I am, believe me," he says. "I'm very focused on you, Miss Foley."

"Good. Then take off your clothes. All of them."

There's a mischievous glint in his eyes, but his body's gone rigid. He might like the idea of this script she's started to write for them, but he also loves being in control. Loves it so much that stripping down in front of her while she sits on his bed a safe distance away, her arms crossed over her chest, has caused his desire to short-circuit for a few seconds.

Slowly, carefully, he unbuckles his belt and unbuttons his jeans. He's taking his sweet time. She figures it's his best attempt to appear calm and indulgent. But she can practically taste his nervousness; she loves the flavor of it as much as she loves the sight of his muscular chest as he peels back the wet flaps of his dress shirt, of his powerful hair-dusted thighs as he tugs his jeans down his legs.

His chest rises and falls with breaths quick and shallow enough to suggest fear. He'd probably like nothing more than to cross the room and tear her clothes from her body, if only to make them equals. But that's not on the syllabus. Not yet.

"Turn around and put your hands on the edge of the table," she says. "Both of them."

He complies. When he realizes he's turned his naked body squarely into the harsh light of the drafting table's lamp, he squints and takes a deep breath to steady himself. But his cock is rising and throbbing. If it's fear he's feeling, in another few seconds, his fear will have him hard as a rock.

When she reaches past him for one of the paintbrushes in the coffee can, he flinches. That's when she's realizes he's kept his eyes closed and her sudden movement has startled him.

"Relax, teach," she whispers. "Everyone's got something to learn."

She sinks to her knees on the floor, sets the brush to one side; she'll need it in a minute if all goes according to plan. But in the meantime, all she needs are her own hands. And her fingers.

"Wh—what are you going to—?"

"No matter what I do," she interrupts him, "keep both hands on the edge of the table and both feet on the floor. The second you let go or step off the floor, we're back to square one."

"And what's square one?"

She hears the slap of her hand against the hard flesh of his ass before she realizes what she's done. She just spanked him. Well, she didn't spank him. She just slapped her former teacher on his bare ass. He lets out a short, startled grunt. She's just as startled as he is. Startled by how quickly and easily she's taken control, by how much the sight of him, in his tall, muscled, nervous glory has filled her with energy and hunger. She feels like she could run a mile without breaking a sweat. It's like her body—no, her *soul*—has taken control of her actions and found the perfect way to exorcise the frightened little girl who ran from him the night before.

Lilliane was right. Crazy, perhaps. But right. She didn't need Bastian Drake's candle at all.

"Square one," she says carefully, her voice shaky with excitement. "Is whatever I say it is."

"You are a bad, bad girl, Laney Foley," he whispers.

"And bad teachers like bad girls," she whispers back. "Both hands on the table."

She starts with just the tips of her fingers, traces swirling patterns over the arches of his bare feet around his hairy ankles, up the sides of his legs. She's memorizing the location of each spot that makes him wince, jerk or shift his weight from one foot to the other. Kneeling on the floor beside him, she monitors the two-handed grip he maintains on the edge of his drafting table as her own fingers slide up the insides of his thighs. He releases a desperate moan when she hops to her feet and he realizes she's skipping his cock and balls. Instead, she allows her fingers to travel the hard ridges of his muscular back.

So far, his most sensitive spots have been the undersides of his biceps and the very back of his neck, so she lingers there, teasing him, testing him, watching his grip on the drafting table turn white-knuckled. Then she sinks to her knees again.

He's mine now. My schedule, my pace, my touch. No rules, no risks, no consequences. Mine.

When her fingers travel the underside of his balls, Michael has to throw his head back and choke out several moans to keep from breaking the rules. So she lingers there too. Back and forth. Back and forth...

"Laney—Jesus. You h-have to—*Laney*."

"Nice job so far," she answers, pulling her hand away. "Now it's time for stage two."

Surrendering to just her fingers has rendered him a sweaty, gasping mess. And while her original intent was solely to learn the most sensitive parts on his body, she realizes this ritual has erased the power deferential between them, whatever the hell *that* is. He was right. She really did read it in a pamphlet. With each inch of his body her fingers have traveled, she's claimed more of her right to desire him as much as he's desired her. Hell, she's claiming her very right to desire, her right to feel lust, to give into it now and then without first jamming it through the ringer of every doubt and fear she can come up with.

The paintbrush is as soft as it looks. The bristles give easily as she drags them gently across Michael's flesh. His struggle now is more intense. He whispers her name every few seconds. She can't tell if they're encouragements or pleas. Either one is more than fine. Then he gasps her name; he groans and growls her name. But he doesn't lift either foot off the floor, he doesn't release his grip on the table even as she paints the underside of his balls with the brush's soft bristles.

He shudders from the assault, teeth gritted, gripping the table's edge, leaning forward far enough that the balls of his feet come up off the floor before he drives them back down again.

Is this an infraction? She thinks not. He's doing so well. He's working so hard. *For her.*

As she squeezes herself into the few inches of space in between him and the desk, she keeps up her soft, silky tease of his balls. Despite being on her knees, she feels as if the power is all hers. Michael looks down at her through squinted eyes, his nostrils flaring, his grunts throaty and pained with desire delayed, frustrated, and enflamed.

"Excellent work, Michael," she whispers. For the first time, she drags the bristles up the length of his jerking shaft.

"Am I, Miss Foley?" he gasps. "Am I doing a good job?"

"Yes," she whispers. She grips the base of his shaft in one hand and sets the brush aside. "You've done a very good job." The tip of his glistening cock is inches from her lips now. The heady, masculine smell of him fills her nostrils.

"Time for stage three," she says.

She's never been this aroused with a man's cock in her mouth before. Blowjobs are usually drudgery or just plain work, something she gives out to dateable guys she's sure will lose interest if she doesn't let them past second base. The idea of feeling this genuinely connected to another man while his cock is down her throat has always seemed like a ridiculous abstraction, something from a romance novel she would never admit to reading. Despite his curses and his pleas, Michael still hasn't let go of the drafting table right behind her. He's still following her rules.

"Laney," he cries.

He's asking her for permission. She's not quite sure for what, but when his cock jerks in the hand she's using to assist her lips, she gets an idea. He's close. He must be. And he's using her name as a warning. If she's not careful, he'll unleash his seed inside of her in another few seconds. Her sudden hunger for it makes her head spin. She's never let someone cum in her mouth before. But she wants him to. She really wants him to. But it's too soon. Worse, it's unsafe in ways that have nothing to do with domination and control. But tell that to her sudden hunger for every part of him, a hunger that makes recklessness feel like strength.

"Laney," he cries.

She pulls him from her mouth. "Do it," she says before she can think twice. "Do it now."

He doesn't come.

He releases the table instead, twines his fingers through her hair, grips the back of her head in one hand, smoothes her tangled bangs back from her forehead with the other. He's staring down at her, studying her with parted lips as she works him over. He didn't want permission to come down her throat. He wanted permission to be released from the rules of her game. Permission to touch, to hold, to caress, to gaze and study.

Suddenly she's on her feet and they're moving toward the bed. He's undressing her with swift precision and an absence of frenzy, each movement governed by the total focus wrought by absolute desire.

By the time he sends her backward down onto the bed, she's naked, the silky comforter kissing her thighs and back as he bears down on her, reaching for the nightstand drawer, tearing the condom wrapper open with his teeth. She's seen so many erections flag during this pivotal step in the process; given the guys they belonged to that wasn't always such a bad thing. But Michael is so hard his cock won't stop jerking long enough for him to slide the condom on. So they both sit there for a few seconds, their rasping breaths fighting with the sounds of the rain pelting the windows. The sight of him sitting on his bent knees, shadows painting the slope of his upper back, steadying his cock with one hand while sliding the condom on with the other makes her lips ache. He's blocking the desk lamp now so she can't tell if her thighs are actually shaking, but it feels like they are. It feels like she's shaking down to her bones as she feels herself opening for him before he even touches her pussy.

"Michael," she whispers.

Gently, he pushes her back into the pillows, his lips inches from hers. He stares into her eyes and he licks the tips of his fingers, holds her gaze while he swirls his moistened fingers around her right nipple. "Yes, Laney."

"Fuck me."

It's not a challenge. It's not a dare. It's not a porn-star snarl. She's never given permission in this simple and direct way before in her life. It's always been, *Yes, I'm ready*, or worse, *Sure, go ahead.* What she's just given him is more than permission. This is beyond simple consent. This is a promise, an offering to match his raw desire with her own.

At first, she thinks he's hesitating because he's still staring into her eyes. Then she feels him pressing against her moist entrance and she realizes he wants, once more, to watch every wave of pleasure ripple through her expression. He wants to turn her into a work of art by fucking her. She's so hot, wet, and open, he smiles and lets out a small, satisfied laugh of surprise. She realizes how much she's given her body over to him when she feels her ankles meet against the small of his back.

"*Need you*," she gasps. "*Need you, Michael.*"

These words make her feel more vulnerable than anything else she's done all night, or all week.

"Need me, want me," he growls. "Take your pick. I'm yours."

He finds her clit with one hand, rubs circles around it while keeping his thrusts varied in a rhythm she can't predict. The knowledge that she's on her back beneath him seems more philosophical than real. She feels boneless suddenly, and that can only mean one thing. She's astonished her orgasm snuck up on her this quickly. She feels as if she's been filled by it an instant. That's never happened to her before. There have always been false starts, sputtering engines. Waves of pleasure that seemed to break just short of the shore. But now Michael fucks her hard and deep, and she feels like she's about to fly apart. This is the moment when another guy would desperately jackhammer into some porn film imitation of a female orgasm. But Michael's learned enough about her body to know it's the combination of his cock's suddenly steady thrusts and the way he's circling her clit with his fingers that have done her in.

She starts by trying to say his name, but this vain attempt turns into a series of cries that have too many emotions swirling through them to be defined. Somewhere in the midst of her bliss, he's pulled free of her. He's suckling her clit while stroking himself at the same time, making her feel worshiped and serviced even amidst her near-delirium. She places her hands gently against his shoulders to let him know she can't take any more, that her body's fully spent. That's when he rises up onto his haunches, brings their mouths together. She grips the back of his neck but at the same instant she fears her nails have dug into his skin, he yanks the condom off, and comes all over her stomach, his seed hot and copious.

He crumples against her as his barking groans turn into delighted laughter.

And for a while there's only the sound of the rain and the gentle feel of his fingers smoothing back her bangs. This is going to be his thing, she can tell. Brushing her hair back from her forehead. And the fact that he's going to have a *thing* that involves her hair makes his expansive bed's embrace feel all the more safe.

"Now you have to lie with me for a night," he says. "Isn't that how it works?"

"How what works?" she asks.

"If you'd used the candle, I mean. Isn't that how the story went?"

"I think it was just a story."

"Maybe, maybe not."

"It doesn't matter," she says.

"Why?"

"Because the only thing I need is—" His embrace tightens even as her words suddenly leave her.

How could her old fears return in this moment, after the amazing night they've shared? Hadn't she done enough to chase her fears away forever?

Maybe that wasn't how this worked. Maybe there was no one thing or one act that could make your fears go away forever. The best you could do was to wake up each day and make a resolution to ignore fear's invitations to false comfort and illusory safety—its invitation to say less, risk less, to love less, to be less. It was a daily decision, being willing to fall in love, and now it was hers to make. That's why she rolled over and took Michael Brouchard's face in her hands, staring into his expectant gaze as she finished the sentence that had lodged in her throat only seconds before.

"The only thing I need is you, Michael Brouchard."

14

LILLIANE

"What's a pretty lady like you doing crying in the rain?" The doorman had watched her approach and pulled open the door when she was a few steps from the entrance to the Hotel Montelone.

Jerry is Lilliane's favorite doorman, probably because his constant flirting makes her feel young in spirit as well as body.

"Who says I'm crying?" Lilliane says, trying to effect her brightest tone.

"You's missing a skip in your step, that's all."

"The rain makes everybody look like they're crying, baby."

He holds open the door as she closes her umbrella, then together they step into the chandelier-lit, marble-floored lobby with its proud grandfather clock and huge, colorful bouquets on every surface. The Carousel Bar is packed as always, spilling a constant stream of drunken laughter onto the short set of carpeted steps just inside the hotel's entrance.

"Not good for you to be walking alone out in this kinda rain, Miss Davis," Jerry says, taking her arm and leading her up the steps, even though there are only a few of them and they're more than easily managed by a woman of any age.

She's been using this alias at the Montelone for almost twenty years now, and soon she'll have to come up with another or start avoiding the hotel altogether. She doesn't run this kind of risk at the other businesses in New Orleans she's fond of; she'll typically frequent them for five years or so before hanging back and waiting for management and most of the staff to get replaced. But here she's gone with baggier dresses, hats with veils and bigger sunglasses. Eventually, even those will fail to do the trick and some of the hotel's long-term staff members will start to wonder why one of their regular guests hasn't aged a day in years. But tonight, just the thought of saying good-bye to the Montelone, even if it's only for a little while, is more than she can bear.

"Well, Jerry, maybe next time you'll have to escort me on my walk."

"That would be an honor, Miss Davis. If I'm not working, that is."

"I'm a guest here, am I not? Are tending to my needs not considered part of your job?"

"Miss Davis. Meeting any of your needs would be my utmost priority. Even if I didn't work at the Montelone."

"You dawg," she whispers, slapping him lightly on the shoulder. His broad, toothy grin has as much charm as desire in it.

"Front desk has something for you, ma'am," he says.

"What is it?"

"I don't know. But it's been here a while. They forgot to give it to you when you checked in."

"Thank you, Jerry."

As she crosses the lobby, she wonders if this is some new trick of Bastian's. Maybe he feels guilty for her abandoning her in the rain. But for that to be the case, he'd have to feel suddenly guilty for fifty-six years of abandoning her whenever she posed a question he couldn't or wouldn't answer. The front desk clerk sees her coming, smiles, reaches under the desk and hands her a tiny envelope with her first initial written on the outside. Like so many of the new hires, the clerk has a thick European accent Lilliane can't quite place.

"Who left this?" Lilliane asks, trying to sound casual.

"I'm not sure, madam. I wasn't on duty at the time. But I do know that it was weeks ago and we informed her that you were not in residence at the time."

"*Her*. Did you tell her I would return?"

"I'm sure we didn't. That would be strictly against policy. But according to my manager, she didn't need us to. She was confident that you would be back eventually and insisted that we give it to you the minute you returned."

"I see. Thank you."

It's not in the same cursive as the notes attached to the candles in

Bastian's shop, but it looks vaguely familiar.

There are only twenty-three people who know she stays here on a regular basis—twenty-four if you count a ghost named Bastian Drake—and all of them could get in touch with her by phone. No need to send a mysterious handwritten note and wait weeks for it to be delivered.

In the past, she's used the hotel for numerous meetings related to The Desire Exchange, so it's possible an old client is trying to track her down. But former clients are all provided with her contact information as well as phone numbers for several of the other Radiants who oversee applications. The Desire Exchange subsists off the referrals. If former clients had to jump through a dozen hoops to make them, The Exchange's profit margins would shrink considerably.

Lilliane knows she should wait until she's comfortably ensconced in her suite. But the Desire Exchange's recent infiltration by a determined young woman and her Navy SEAL lover has her more than a little on edge when it comes to messages from strangers.

As the elevator rises, she tears open the envelope. Her eyes dart immediately to the unfamiliar phone number written across the bottom of the card inside. The penmanship is another story. At first, it seems only vaguely familiar. Then, recognition; she hasn't laid eyes on the person responsible for these pen strokes in at least five years.

When she finally looks up from the message written on the card, she realizes the strangers getting onto the elevator are coming from a floor above her own. She's missed her stop entirely and now she's hurrying to shove the card where no one else can see its short, blunt message:

THERE'S A WAY OUT, LILLIANE.
THERE'S A WAY FOR US TO LOVE AGAIN.
CALL ME. PLEASE.

Sign up for the 1001 Dark Nights Newsletter
and be entered to win a Tiffany Key necklace.

There's a contest every month!

Go to www.1001DarkNights.com to subscribe.

As a bonus, all subscribers will receive a free
1001 Dark Nights story
The First Night
by Lexi Blake & M.J. Rose

Turn the page for a full list of the
1001 Dark Nights fabulous novellas...

1001 Dark Nights

WICKED WOLF by Carrie Ann Ryan
A Redwood Pack Novella

WHEN IRISH EYES ARE HAUNTING by Heather Graham
A Krewe of Hunters Novella

EASY WITH YOU by Kristen Proby
A With Me In Seattle Novella

MASTER OF FREEDOM by Cherise Sinclair
A Mountain Masters Novella

CARESS OF PLEASURE by Julie Kenner
A Dark Pleasures Novella

ADORED by Lexi Blake
A Masters and Mercenaries Novella

HADES by Larissa Ione
A Demonica Novella

RAVAGED by Elisabeth Naughton
An Eternal Guardians Novella

DREAM OF YOU by Jennifer L. Armentrout
A Wait For You Novella

STRIPPED DOWN by Lorelei James
A Blacktop Cowboys ® Novella

RAGE/KILLIAN by Alexandra Ivy/Laura Wright
Bayou Heat Novellas

DRAGON KING by Donna Grant
A Dark Kings Novella

PURE WICKED by Shayla Black
A Wicked Lovers Novella

HARD AS STEEL by Laura Kaye
A Hard Ink/Raven Riders Crossover

STROKE OF MIDNIGHT by Lara Adrian
A Midnight Breed Novella

ALL HALLOWS EVE by Heather Graham
A Krewe of Hunters Novella

KISS THE FLAME by Christopher Rice
A Desire Exchange Novella

DARING HER LOVE by Melissa Foster
A Bradens Novella

TEASED by Rebecca Zanetti
A Dark Protectors Novella

THE PROMISE OF SURRENDER by Liliana Hart
A MacKenzie Family Novella

FOREVER WICKED by Shayla Black
A Wicked Lovers Novella

CRIMSON TWILIGHT by Heather Graham
A Krewe of Hunters Novella

CAPTURED IN SURRENDER by Liliana Hart
A MacKenzie Family Novella

SILENT BITE: A SCANGUARDS WEDDING by Tina Folsom
A Scanguards Vampire Novella

DUNGEON GAMES by Lexi Blake
A Masters and Mercenaries Novella

AZAGOTH by Larissa Ione
A Demonica Novella

NEED YOU NOW by Lisa Renee Jones
A Shattered Promises Series Prelude

SHOW ME, BABY by Cherise Sinclair
A Masters of the Shadowlands Novella

ROPED IN by Lorelei James
A Blacktop Cowboys ® Novella

TEMPTED BY MIDNIGHT by Lara Adrian
A Midnight Breed Novella

THE FLAME by Christopher Rice
A Desire Exchange Novella

CARESS OF DARKNESS by Julie Kenner
A Dark Pleasures Novella

Also from Evil Eye Concepts:

TAME ME by J. Kenner
A Stark International Novella

THE SURRENDER GATE By Christopher Rice
A Desire Exchange Novel

SERVICING THE TARGET By Cherise Sinclair
A Masters of the Shadowlands Novel

Bundles:

BUNDLE ONE
Includes:
Forever Wicked by Shayla Black
Crimson Twilight by Heather Graham
Captured in Surrender by Liliana Hart
Silent Bite by Tina Folsom

BUNDLE TWO
Includes:
Dungeon Games by Lexi Blake
Azagoth by Larissa Ione
Need You Now by Lisa Renee Jones
Show My, Baby by Cherise Sinclair

BUNDLE THREE
Includes:
Roped In by Lorelei James
Tempted By Midnight by Lara Adrian
The Flame by Christopher Rice
Caress of Darkness by Julie Kenner

About Christopher Rice

New York Times bestselling author Christopher Rice's first foray into erotic romance, *THE FLAME*, earned accolades from some of the genre's most beloved authors. "Sensual, passionate and intelligent," wrote Lexi Blake, "it's everything an erotic romance should be." J. Kenner called it "absolutely delicious," Cherise Sinclair hailed it as "beautifully lyrical" and Lorelei James announced, "I look forward to reading more!"*KISS THE FLAME:* A Desire Exchange Novella will be available this November from 1,001 DARK NIGHTS. Before his erotic romance debut, Christopher published four *New York Times* bestselling thrillers before the age of 30, received a Lambda Literary Award and was declared one of People Magazine's Sexiest Men Alive. His supernatural thriller, *THE HEAVENS RISE*, was a nominated for a Bram Stoker Award. Together with his best friend, *New York Times* bestselling author Eric Shaw Quinn, Christopher co-hosts and executive produces THE DINNER PARTY SHOW WITH CHRISTOPHER RICE & ERIC SHAW QUINN which debuts a new episode every Sunday evening at 8 PM ET/ 5 PM PT at TheDinnerPartyShow.com.

Dance of Desire

By Christopher Rice
Coming February 23, 2016

From *New York Times* bestselling author Christopher Rice, comes a steamy, emotional tale of forbidden romance between a woman struggling to get her life on its feet and the gorgeous cowboy her father kept her from marrying years before. The first contemporary romance from Christopher Rice is written with the author's trademark humor and heart, and introduces readers to a beautiful town in the Texas Hill Country called Chapel Springs.

* * * *

"It's a terrible idea," he says.

"Why did she tell you?"

"Because she wants me to stop you."

"That's not true. I talked to her this afternoon and she told me she wanted me to go."

"Well, she must have changed her mind," he says.

"Well, I haven't changed mine."

"A sex club?" he bellows. "What are you? Crazy?"

"Since when are you so full of judgment, cowboy? I've never seen you in church!"

"And I've never seen you in a sex club!"

"Have you been to that many? Who knows? I could have a whole secret life you don't even know about."

"I know who you are, Amber. I know *how* you are."

"And what does that mean?"

"Amber, you stayed a virgin until you were nineteen. That puts you in the, like, one percentile of girls in our high school."

"How do you know that? I never told you that!"

"I had my sources."

"You were keeping tabs on my virginity? That's rich. I thought you were too busy starting fistfights outside the Valley View Mall so you didn't have to feel anything."

"And you were too busy tending to my wounds 'cause it gave you an excuse to look at my chest."

"Get out of my house!"

"Amber—"

"Get out!"

He bows his head. A lesser man would ignore her request, but he knows he's bound by it.

"I shouldn't have said that," Caleb whispers. "I'm sorry."

He turns to leave.

"You know, I forgave you a lot because you lost a lot. But don't you pretend for one second that you joined our family with a smile and a thank you and that was that. Those first few years, it was like living with a tornado. You were *impossible!* An you were nothing like the guy I'd..."

He turns away from the front door. "The guy you'd what?"

"All I'm saying is that even if I'd wanted to…"

"Wanted to what?"

He's closing the distance between them. Her head wants to run from him. Her soul wants to run to him. Her body's forced to split the difference. She's got no choice but to stand there while he advances on her, nostrils flaring, blue eyes blazing.

"Tell me why you really don't want me to go," she hears herself whisper. "Tell me why you—"

He takes her in his arms and rocks them into the wall, so suddenly she expects her head to knock against the wood, but one of his powerful hands cushions the back of her skull just in time.

His lips meet the nape of her neck, grazing, testing. It's hesitant, the kiss he gives her there, as if he's afraid she's an apparition that will vanish if he tries to take a real taste.

He gathers the hem of her shirt into his fist, knuckles grazing the skin of her stomach. She's trying to speak but the only thing coming out of her are stuttering gasps. She's been rendered wordless by the feel of the forbidden, by the weight of the forbidden, by the power of the forbidden.

It's the first time they've touched since that night on the boat dock, if you don't include the light dabs of hydrogen peroxide she'd apply to the wounds he got fighting, usually while they sat together in the kitchen, her parents watching over them nervously. Twelve years living under the same roof and they never shared so much as a hug after that night, nothing that might risk the feel of his skin against her own.

And now this.

Now the intoxicating blend of the cologne he wore as a teenager mingling with the musky aroma of his belt and boots. Now the knowledge that he'd asked after her virginity years before, that the thought of her lying with another man had filled him with protective, jealous rage then just as it does now.

She feels boneless and moist. One of those feelings isn't an illusion.

If this is what it feels like to be bad, she thinks, *no wonder so many people get addicted.*

"Tell me," she whispers. "Tell me why you really don't want me to go."

"I am," he growls.

He presses their foreheads together, takes the sides of her face in both of his large, powerful hands. It's torture, this position. It's deliberate, she's sure. It keeps her from lifting her mouth to his. Keeps her from looking straight into his eyes. He's fighting it, still. Just as she's fought it for years.

She parts her lips, inviting him to kiss her.

"Please," he groans. "Just, please *don't* go."

"Caleb…" She reaches for his face.

Welcome to Storm, Texas, where passion runs hot, desire runs deep, and secrets have the power to destroy...

Nestled among rolling hills and painted with vibrant wildflowers, the bucolic town of Storm, Texas, seems like nothing short of perfection.

But there are secrets beneath the facade. Dark secrets. Powerful secrets. The kind that can destroy lives and tear families apart. The kind that can cut through a town like a tempest, leaving jealousy and destruction in its wake, along with shattered hopes and broken dreams. All it takes is one little thing to shatter that polish.

Reading like an on-going drama in the tradition of classic day and night-time soap operas like Dallas, Dynasty, and All My Children, *Rising Storm* is full of scandal, deceit, romance, passion, and secrets.

With 1001 Dark Nights as the "producer," Julie Kenner and Dee Davis use a television model with each week building on the last to create a storyline that fulfills the promise of a drama-filled soap opera. Joining Kenner and Davis in the "writer's room" is an incredible group of *New York Times* bestselling authors such as Lexi Blake, Elisabeth Naughton, Jennifer Probst, Larissa Ione, Rebecca Zanetti and Lisa Mondello who have brought their vision of Storm to life.

A serial soap opera containing eight episodes in season one, the season premiere of *Rising Storm,* TEMPEST RISING, debuts September 24th with each subsequent episode releasing consecutively this fall.

So get ready. The storm is coming.

Experience Rising Storm Here… http://risingstormbooks.com

On behalf of 1001 Dark Nights,

Liz Berry and M.J. Rose would like to thank ~

Steve Berry
Doug Scofield
Kim Guidroz
Jillian Stein
InkSlinger PR
Dan Slater
Asha Hossain
Chris Graham
Pamela Jamison
Jessica Johns
Dylan Stockton
Richard Blake
BookTrib After Dark
The Dinner Party Show
and Simon Lipskar

CPSIA information can be obtained
at www.ICGtesting.com
Printed in the USA
LVOW12s2354211117
557260LV00001B/77/P

9 781940 887753